"Do we really have to talk about your sister and my brother?"

Nick smiled at Joy. "I'd much rather talk about you."

"There's nothing about me to talk about." Joy turned back to the counter.

"We could talk about whether you've been affected by the sun or any full moons since I've been gone."

Joy's face flushed deep red. Was he intentionally trying to embarrass her by bringing up that long-ago kiss?

Dear Reader,

This month Silhouette Romance has six irresistible novels for you, starting with our FABULOUS FATHERS selection, *Mad for the Dad* by Terry Essig. When a sexy single man becomes an instant dad to a toddler, the independent divorcée next door offers parenthood lessons—only to dream of marriage and motherhood all over again!

In *Having Gabriel's Baby* by Kristin Morgan, our BUNDLES OF JOY book, a fleeting night of passion with a handsome, brooding rancher leaves Joelle in the family way—and the dad-to-be insisting on a marriage of convenience for the sake of the baby....

Years ago Julie had been too young for the dashing man of her dreams. Now he's back in town, and Julie's still hoping he'll make her his bride in *New Year's Wife* by Linda Varner, part of her miniseries HOME FOR THE HOLIDAYS.

What's a man to do when he has no interest in marriage but is having trouble resisting the lovely, warm and wonderful woman in his life? Get those cold feet to the nearest wedding chapel in *Family Addition* by Rebecca Daniels.

In *About That Kiss* by Jayne Addison, Joy Mackey, sister of the bride, is sure her sis's ex-fiancé has returned to sabotage the wedding. But his intention is to walk down the aisle with Joy!

And finally, when a woman shows up on a bachelor doctor's doorstep with a baby that looks just like him, everyone in town mistakenly thinks the tiny tot is his in Christine Scott's *Groom on the Loose*.

Enjoy!

Melissa Senate, Senior Editor

Please address questions and book requests to:
Silhouette Reader Service
U.S.: 3010 Walden Ave., P.O. Box 1325, Buffalo, NY 14269
Canadian: P.O. Box 609, Fort Erie, Ont. L2A 5X3

ABOUT THAT KISS

Jayne Addison

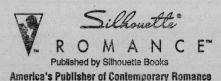

R O M A N C E™
Published by Silhouette Books
America's Publisher of Contemporary Romance

To Evelyn, Rochelle, Lara and Beth.

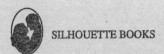 SILHOUETTE BOOKS

ISBN 0-373-19202-9

ABOUT THAT KISS

Copyright © 1997 by Jane Atkin

Books by Jayne Addison

Silhouette Romance

You Made Me Love You #888
*Something Blue #944
*A Precious Gift #980
*Temporary Groom #1034
Wild West Wife #1117
About That Kiss #1202

*The Falco Family

JAYNE ADDISON

lives on the north shore of Long Island with her husband, Jerry. Their three children, Steven, Andrew and Beth, are presently attending colleges away from home. Jayne finds that writing romance fiction is a great way to beat the empty-nest syndrome. When Jayne isn't writing, reading or on the phone, you can find her at her local video store checking out the rentals. Needless to say, romance flicks are her favorites.

Long Island and environs

Prologue

Joy Mackey squared her slim shoulders and brought her hand up to knock on Nick Tremain's apartment door. But she didn't knock. Instead she fanned herself with her hand. She felt very warm, though it wasn't particularly hot for Long Island in July, no more than eighty degrees and not at all humid yet at nine o'clock in the morning. The heat she was feeling had nothing to do with the temperature. She was about to do something she knew she probably shouldn't be doing. Not that it was going to stop her from doing it.

Joy drew in a deep breath, then turned on her heels in a complete about-face. She walked four straight steps away from the door. Then two more steps right to the outdoor railing of his third-story, motel-style unit. She'd carefully planned what she was going to say on the drive over from Greenport. Now she couldn't remember her great opening line.

"Hi, Nick..." Joy practiced, going for a breezy tone.

"Hi, Joy," Nick replied, as he opened his front door.

Surprised, Joy spun around to face him. "Hi, Nick," Joy repeated, still startled.

"Hi, again." Nick closed the door behind him and stood with her in the covered walkway that was open to the elements.

Joy had recovered her composure sufficiently to deliver what she considered her friendliest smile. "Are you going somewhere?" She took note of his white T-shirt lauding the New York Jets, blue jean cutoffs with white strings dangling onto his rugged thighs. His bare feet were in well-worn sneakers and set wide apart at the moment.

"A walk on the beach." His blue eyes made a quick trip over her own casual attire. But they lingered on her bare legs, she noticed.

"Okay," Joy said brightly, matching his stride as he headed for the stairs.

"I suppose that means you're coming with me," Nick stated.

"Yes." Joy stuck her chin out stubbornly.

"Did Diana send you?"

"No. My sister did not send me."

"Does she know you're here?"

"No." Joy shook her head emphatically, gesturing flamboyantly with both her hands. "I'm here on my own."

Frowning, Nick said, "Let me tell you right now, I don't want to talk about it."

Joy gritted her teeth. "I'll talk. You just have to listen."

"I don't suppose you're going to give me any choice."

Since he obviously knew what she was here for, Joy launched right in. "I can't believe how ridiculous the two of you are being. You and Diana love each other. There has to be a way for you to work this out. No one decides to get married and then breaks up in the same day."

Joy looked at his face to see what reaction she'd garnered. The glance he returned was totally impassive. She'd been told she was stubborn a number of times in her life. She was even willing to admit to it. But in this instance, Nick took the prize.

Without commenting, Nick led the way to the street and held the door for her. Squinting her gray-green eyes against the more direct sunlight, Joy walked out, Nick right behind her.

He took a short path up a dune and then down to the beach. There were very few people around—joggers mostly. That's the way it usually was on a Thursday morning. The New York City crowd hit the beach only on weekends.

"You're not saying anything," Joy pointed out, having to raise her voice. He'd gotten ahead of her. The sand was getting into her open sandals, slowing her steps.

Nick stopped and turned. "I already told you that I don't want to talk about it." He watched her trying to shake the sand from her shoes. The hint of an easy smile came across his mouth. "Why don't you just take them off?"

"Will you wait for me?" Joy studied him measuringly, wondering if he'd jog off and deliberately leave her behind.

This time when Nick smiled it was a full-fledged grin. "I'll wait for you."

Joy bent over to undo the ties of her sandals. It was the first time she'd worn them. The single bow hadn't held when she'd put them on so she'd doubled it. Now she was having a hard time getting the knot open. Joy straightened up and ran her moist palms and fingers down the sides of her shorts. Then she bent over to tackle the knot again.

Nick walked over and stood directly in front of her. He drew his key chain out from the pocket of his shorts and squatted. "Put your foot up here." He tapped his right thigh. "Let me see what I can do."

Joy saw the silver flash of a small pocketknife as he released it from his key chain. "I don't want you to cut them off." She met his upward glance with a horrific look. "I just bought them yesterday. They're not as comfortable as I thought they'd be, but I still like how they look."

"I like how they look, too," Nick quipped, his tone sexy. "Give me your foot. I'm just going to use the tip of the knife to loosen the knot."

Joy knew he was only being teasingly flirtatious, but her face was flushed as she placed her foot on his thigh and gripped his hard shoulder to balance herself. Inadvertently her fingertips touched his thick, dark hair, which was a little long at the back of his neck. The combination of its soft silkiness and the strength of his muscles made her shiver. His gaze met hers just then, and Joy was suddenly extremely embarrassed that he'd somehow guessed she'd just experienced an unquestionably sexual reaction. She wasn't supposed to have that kind of a reaction to Nick.

Joy turned her head aside and tried to appear blasé. She gathered up her rust-colored hair from the back of her neck, holding the wavy mass up for a few seconds before letting it drop down to her shoulders again. She was overly conscious of Nick's hand around her ankle. And though she could feel the direct warmth of the sun, she was still shivering inside. She had the sudden urge to hum a tune—something bouncy and distracting.

"Give me your other foot," Nick said, having freed her of one sandal without Joy even realizing it.

Joy made the switch after letting the opened sandal slide off her foot and onto the sand. She pictured Diana and Nick as a couple. They were like a matched set of bookends. They both had almost pitch-black hair and blue eyes. He was unequivocally good-looking. Diana was unbelievably beautiful. They were so right for each other.

Nick made faster work out of the second knot. Joy let go of his firm shoulder as she shook off her other sandal. Holding her shoes together by their strings, she curled her bare toes into the sand beneath her feet.

"How did you get that small scar under your chin?" Nick asked, getting to his feet.

"I fell out of a tree when I was eight years old."

"A tomboy, huh?"

"I guess," Joy conceded. "My mother told me that when I left the house she always worried about me coming back in one piece. Diana always complained about having to watch me even when we were in our teens."

"My brother, Kevin, always got stuck baby-sitting me, too. I was glad I wasn't the older one."

Joy nodded her head in agreement. "I know you're thirty-one. How much older is Kevin?" She'd met his brother once. Kevin was a lawyer with a successful practice here in East Hampton. The two men didn't look any more alike than she looked like Diana. Joy did remember Kevin Tremain being nice-looking in his own right, but minus his brother's lawless charisma.

"He's four years older. Diana is three years older than you, right?"

"Yes," Joy answered. "I used to feel so bad when Diana would get punished along with me for all the scrapes I'd get into." Joy thought about the small scar high up on her left thigh. She had mastered skate-boarding—eventually.

Nick wiggled his eyebrows and gave her a wide grin. "How about we match scrapes? You show me yours. I'll show you mine."

Joy shook her head impatiently. "I know what you're doing. You're trying to get me off track. I want to talk about you and Diana and the way you both are right now...which is miserable."

"How about telling me what idea you've come up with for your next column?"

They'd talked about the column she wrote for her town's local paper quite a few times. It was the flip side of his photojournalism career.

She exhaled with great exasperation. "Please, Nick... This is Diana's and your future. You've got to work it out."

"That's not fair," Nick told her.

"What's not fair?" Joy eyed him, baffled.

"The way you say *please* is hard on a guy."

"Come on, Nick. Ple-e-eze." Joy admonished his playful ploy with an aggravated look.

Nick sighed. "Do you want to walk?"

"No. I want to stand here and have this out with you." Joy peered up at him adamantly. "I know there's a compromise the two of you can reach. I don't think Diana is right to expect you to change your career from a photojournalist to a commercial photographer, and I don't think Diana is right not to be willing to meet you partway and curtail all the buying trips she's always running off on for her clients. I know the two of you can find a way to have quality time together. You can't break up over this!"

"Maybe Diana and I only thought we had a future together." He'd had three days now to examine his feelings, and he'd come up with some serious second thoughts that had nothing to do with either one of their careers.

"You and Diana do have a future together," Joy continued assertively. "I know Diana will compromise on her end if the two of you just talk it out."

Nick folded his arms across his chest. "You know what I realized a little while ago?"

"What?"

"I've had longer conversations with you than I've ever had with Diana."

It took Joy a second to respond. "When two people are in love they don't need to do that much talking."

"Joy, I really would like you to drop this."

But she would not be deterred. "This is your quandary. You and Diana didn't talk enough before. Now you have to talk."

Nick unwound his arms and reached out to place a hand lightly on Joy's mouth. But she turned her head just then and his fingers got caught in her hair.

Joy's eyes flew to his face while he untangled his fingers. She gazed at him askance for a second, then went right on. "The way I see it . . ."

The rest of her speech was cut off as Nick captured her face between his hands and out of aggravation covered her mouth with his. He had no thought of doing what he did next, but he'd caught her with her lips parted, and his tongue went where it wanted to go. Spontaneously his hands left her face to bring her up flush against his chest, locking them together in a full-length embrace.

He felt Joy's tongue arch in uncertainty. Then her arms found their way around his neck and she made the fit even better by rising up on her toes. The sandals dropped from her fingers, and she was kissing him back.

Nick fought a desire to touch more of her with his hands, but that didn't stop his enjoyment of her mouth. He had no sense at all of wanting to stop, though he did try for a millisecond to clear his head.

A couple of teenage boys walking by whistled their approval. It was only then that Joy and Nick put an abrupt end to what they were doing.

Joy's arms dropped flaggingly from his neck. Nick let her body slide back down until her heels met the sand before he let go of her. He stared at her.

Joy stared back. *Oh, my! Oh, my!* she thought.

"Whoo!" Nick breathed. "Where did that come from?"

Joy eyed him incredulously. *Where did that come from?*

"I'm sorry," he said. "I don't know what got into me."

"Well...ah." Joy floundered inanely. "What I mean is...well... It's the heat...the sun... The sun can make people do crazy things."

"Right. The sun." Nick stuck his hands in his pockets. "I thought it was a full moon that did that."

"Right. That, too. And the sun." Joy trained her eyes down at the sand. God! She'd been falling in love with Nick while he and Diana had been falling in love with each other. All it had taken was that kiss—that earth-shattering kiss—to make her face the truth.

Joy raised her eyes from the sand, but she didn't meet his gaze head-on. She kept her focus on one neatly trimmed sideburn. "I should be going now. We've talked...and all."

Was her face as red as she thought it was?

"We've talked," Nicked agreed, suddenly subdued.

Joy started to leave. She got four large steps away, when Nick called her.

"Your sandals," he said.

Joy came back. They both bent down at the same time to pick up her shoes. Their fingers accidentally touched and their eyes met briefly. With the speed of lightning Joy jerked her hand away. Nick gathered together her sandals and he extended them to her as they both straightened up.

Joy felt she should make one last comment on Diana's behalf. "I know you're letting your male ego get in your way. Will you stop being so obstinate and marry my sister!"

With that parting remark she walked away. When she looked back over her shoulder she saw Nick standing at the water's edge, watching her retreat.

Chapter One

"Maxie, I am not playing with you in that pile of leaves," Joy complained to the huge mutt. She'd been enjoying a lazy Sunday until the dog's insistence made her go outside.

The mutt pulled at its leash, yanking Joy along.

"Maxie... it's cold out. Let's just get to the woods and do what you made me think you needed to do." She was walking him—though running was probably more accurate—in the rear grounds of the large, rambling house in Greenport where she still lived with her mother and a series of guests during the summer season. Her mother had turned the house into a bed and breakfast after her father's death three years ago.

Maxie headed straight for the largest pile of leaves on the back lawn and made every attempt to climb to the top of the heap. Joy made every attempt to stop him until she slid on a patch of leaves coated with ice and tumbled into the pile. It was the end of November and the winter-cold air froze any moisture on the ground.

"All right. You want leaves, Maxie," Joy said, laughing as she lay on her back. She let go of the leash, picked up a handful of leaves and threw them up at the dog.

Maxie barked happily.

"Can I play, too?" a voice asked from behind her.

As Joy looked up, her heart lurched, then quickened to a mile a minute. Nick. In an ungainly fashion, discombobulated as she was by his appearance, Joy struggled to get to her feet. Nick came to the rescue and took hold of her wrists to pull her up. Maxie sprang at him, his front paws ploughing into Nick's back.

"What the..." Nick uttered, just before he landed indelicately on top of Joy, his thighs straddling her hips.

Lifting himself enough to balance his weight on his elbows, Nick smiled down at her. "Hi, Joy."

"Nick..." His face was no more than inches from hers. Her heart was beating wildly.

Nick's smile became a grin. "This kind of feels like where we left off the last time we were together."

Joy was breathless just looking up at him without that reminder. Not that she needed any prompting to be reminded. "I—I think we should get up."

A smile still on his mouth, Nick bounced back on his heels. Getting the leverage he needed, he sprang to his feet. Joy grasped his offered hands and got to her feet, noticing that Nick held on to her a touch longer than was necessary.

"What are you doing here?" Joy asked. It was about four and a half months since she'd last seen him. He'd accepted an assignment abroad two days after their morning on the beach. He hadn't been back since.

"Where else would I be with your sister marrying my brother? They haven't changed their minds, have they?" He brushed leaves off her shoulders.

"No, they haven't changed their minds. They're getting married in three weeks. The reception is going to be here in the house." Joy was shivering more from her pulse going wild than from the cold. She was bundled up well enough, in a very heavy sweater, the war-surplus pea coat she wore to knock around in and a knit hat pulled down low on her forehead and covering her ears.

"Diana and Kevin didn't expect you to be able to get back for their wedding." Joy thought in horror about what she must look like to him. The sweater and coat had to make it seem like she'd added fifty pounds to her frame. And that wasn't the worst of it. The hat! The hat was the worst. "You're supposed to be in Europe."

"I was in Europe yesterday. Now I'm here. I did what I had to do to get back."

He thought she looked adorable. Her face was all eyes. The hair at her neck was hidden under the collar of her coat. "I wasn't going to miss my brother's wedding." His first inclination had been to show up after the fact, but only because he was concerned that Kevin would be uneasy. Though when Kevin had called to tell him he was marrying Nick's ex-fiancée, his brother hadn't sounded uneasy.

Joy gazed up at him suspiciously, her eyebrows getting lost under her hat.

"What's that look for?" Nick grinned as he picked out a few leaves that had stuck to her hat. He knew what she was thinking. Only she couldn't have been farther from the truth. He was not in love with Diana. He hadn't thought about her at all during the past four and a half months. He *had* thought a lot about the woman standing in front of him right now.

"You're here to make trouble, right?" Joy nodded her head in emphasis.

"No, I'm not here to make trouble. Scout's honor. Now do I get to come in out of the cold?" He made a point of flippantly hiking up the collar on his leather bomber jacket. The wind was buffeting her back and ruffling his hair. The cold wasn't bothering him, but he expected she was freezing, given the way she was doing a little jig from foot to foot.

"Yes, you get to come in," Joy replied tartly and turned toward the house.

Seeing that she was forgetting her mutt, Nick grabbed the leash and dragged Maxie along as he followed her into the house. Joy went through a back door straight into the inn's large, homey kitchen. Nick unfastened the dog's leash and hung it up on a hook near the door while Maxie took off.

Joy quickly yanked the ugly hat off her head, stuffed it in her coat pocket and tried casually to fluff her soft brown hair with her fingers. "Are you hungry?"

"Starved. I didn't stop for lunch. How about going out with me for something to eat? Did you have lunch?"

"I've had lunch." It was going on four p.m. "I'll make you a couple of sandwiches. There's some cold chicken." Joy unbuttoned her coat and hung it on a peg near the back door. She didn't feel she'd been able to do much with her hair.

"Cold chicken sounds great," Nick said, taking his jacket off and hanging it on a peg alongside hers. "Kevin told me Diana's been staying here till the wedding and that he comes out on the weekend. Did I miss him?"

"No. He'll be back." Joy closed the refrigerator door with the side of her hip. She had a platter of cold chicken and a jar of mayonnaise in her hands. "They went to have lunch with my mother at the restaurant that's doing the catering. They're still debating about some of the dishes they want at the wedding."

"How come you didn't go with them?" He moved to stand next to her at the counter.

Joy looked at him from the corner of her eye. She'd already taken in the lean-hipped fit of his black slacks and the bulky, wheat-toned sweater, that made it impossible not to notice his wide shoulders.

"I'm too much of a junk-food junkie to be on the food committee." She meant to speak in a joking tone, but his nearness was giving her a case of apoplexy. The words came out flat.

His eyes roved over her profile. "What committee are you on?"

"Wedding attire and flowers." Joy took two rolls out of a bakery bag on the counter and a knife from a drawer. "And..." She was about to say more but his hand came up to her hair, ending that train of thought. "What are you doing?"

"Smoothing down your hair," Nick said easily. "Turn around and let me get the other side."

Joy swung around to face him. She was secretly thrilled by his attention, which was exactly what had her bristling now. "You know what surprises me?"

"What surprises you?" He took the knife she didn't realize she was still holding out of her hand and put it down on the counter.

"I'm surprised that you didn't come back when Diana and Kevin first started dating." Joy watched his gaze drop to her hips as she placed her hands there. For a second Joy wondered if she was intentionally trying to flatten her red sweater so he'd know it was the sweater that was puffy, not her hips.

"Actually I didn't know Diana and Kevin were dating. The first I heard of them being a couple was when Kevin got ahold of me and told me they were getting married. But I wouldn't have come back even if I had known."

My eye! Joy muttered in her head. He certainly had come back quickly enough when he'd found out they were getting married.

"Do we really have to talk about Diana and Kevin?" He smiled. "I'd much rather talk about you."

"There's nothing about me to talk about." Joy turned back to the counter. She picked up the knife and jaggedly sliced open both rolls.

"We could talk about your column. Or we could talk about whether you've been affected by the sun or any full moons since I've been gone."

Joy's face flushed deep red. Was he intentionally trying to embarrass her by bringing up that kiss? "Did Kevin tell you how he and Diana first got together?"

"No and I didn't ask," Nick responded disinterestedly.

"Diana needed a lawyer to collect money from one of her clients," Joy said. "That was three months ago."

Nick leaned back against the counter. "I assume Kevin got Diana's client to fork over."

Joy nodded. Taking a plate down from the cabinet overhead she placed the sandwiches on top of it. "He's a very good lawyer."

"No question about that." Nick took the plate and walked over to the kitchen table in the center of the room.

Joy made a half turn in his direction. "Would you like a beer with that?"

"Okay." Nick took a seat and stretched his legs out.

Joy came to the table with a glass, a bottle of beer and a bag of potato chips. She placed her bounty down within his reach and then took a seat across from him.

Nick opened the bag of chips, took a helping out and put them on his plate. He passed the bag to her. Joy took a handful of chips out for herself.

She watched him begin eating his sandwich.

He watched her munch on chips.

A stretch without any conversation went by while Joy commanded herself to get her eyes off him. Her command went unheeded.

Nick finished one sandwich. "How are you doing with your column?" He had read them all, having

worked out an arrangement with the owner/editor of
the *Greenport News* to have the paper forwarded to
him. He'd even spoken to her editor a few times,
which was how he'd known the paper was up for sale
before any official announcement. He toyed with the
idea of telling her that he was her new boss, instead of
waiting until tomorrow at the Monday morning staff
meeting.

"It's going okay," Joy returned. "Nothing all that
exciting." She did have something exciting in the
works, but she didn't want to go off on that tangent
now. She was hoping to ease back into the topic of
Diana and Kevin. She wanted a more definitive expression from him about his intent.

"You're the one with the glamorous career," Joy
said, directing the conversation to his globetrotting.
She knew he'd been in Russia, Egypt, then Europe
during the past four and a half months. She'd hunted
out every picture of his that had been published.

"It's not at all glamorous. Living out of a back-
pack most of the time means not always showering.
And it's almost impossible to establish any relationships. As soon as I meet someone I'd like to get to
know, I'm off to someplace else."

Joy tipped her head slightly. "That doesn't sound
at all like the way you used to speak about your career."

Nick shrugged his shoulders.

Joy was surprised by his change of attitude. It was
the excitement she used to hear in his voice that had
given her the impetus to seek out a similar career for
herself as a journalist. She'd just gotten a go-ahead
last Friday to take on an assignment in Bolivia, three

days after Diana and Kevin's wedding. She hadn't told anyone about it yet. She thought it only right that she give her notice in to the *Greenport News* first.

Joy dabbed up some potato chip crumbs on the table with the tip of her finger. "That part about not getting a chance to really know people you wanted to get to know, did that include women you might have thought of getting serious with?"

"Are you asking me if I was interested in anyone romantically?"

"Was that what it sounded like?" She'd been trying to find out whether there had been any lessening in his feelings for Diana. It wasn't because she was jealous, she reminded herself.

"That's what it sounded like," Nick said, grinning. He poured beer into his glass, then studied her over the rim as he took a deep swallow.

"So were you?" Joy impatiently met the mirthful look in his eyes.

Maxie barked just as the front door opened.

Joy took a big frustrated breath and blew it out fast, releasing her disappointment that there wasn't time now to press him for a response.

Nick's gaze locked with hers. "No, I didn't meet any woman I wanted to spend more than one night with or even a single night with."

"Oh," Joy managed to say, before her mother appeared in the kitchen, followed by Diana and Kevin. All three looked as surprised to see Nick as Joy had been.

"Nick..." Emily Mackey gushed. She was an attractively unfussy woman on the cusp of turning fifty. Short brown hair framed her lively round face. "It's wonderful to see you again. We couldn't imagine whose car was in the driveway.''

''It's wonderful to see you,'' Nick said, returning the smile. He was on his feet, enthusiastically ready to receive a hug, bending to accommodate Emily, who was inches shorter than both her daughters.

Kevin approached to shake his hand, then thump him on the back, getting a thump in return from Nick as males will do in place of an embrace.

''Son of a gûn,'' Kevin said with a grin almost identical to the grin he was getting from Nick. ''I thought you still had pictures to take.''

''I couldn't think of any picture I wanted to take more than one of you getting hog-tied.'' Nick raised his eyebrows, relieved to see that Kevin appeared really happy he'd arrived.

Then it was Nick and Diana facing each other as Kevin drew Diana to his side.

''Hi, Nick,'' Diana said slowly.

''Diana,'' Nick replied without a grin. He hoped she was truly in love with Kevin. She was going to have him to answer to if his brother got hurt.

Joy caught the lingering look between Nick and Diana and glanced quickly at Kevin to check for his take on the situation. Kevin's brown eyes gazed affectionately—and naively—at Diana. Joy resisted an impulse to punch Kevin in the head.

''Joy, did you put on coffee?'' Emily Mackey asked, taking off her coat, adding it to the leather jacket and navy pea coat already on hooks.

''No, but I will,'' she replied. Joy watched Diana and Nick break their regard of each other, and she walked over to the counter where the coffee maker was.

Filling the pot with water, Joy observed as Kevin assisted Diana with her coat. Joy already knew what Diana was wearing underneath her coat. A short, straight black skirt, a white cashmere sweater, black tights and sexy black high-heeled boots.

Joy craned her neck to see if Nick was appraising her sister. When she saw that Diana did indeed have his attention—Joy let the water spill out over the top of the glass coffeepot. Embarrassed she quickly turned off the faucet.

Kevin said to his brother, "I know you gave up your lease. You'll stay with me."

"Thanks, Kev," Nick replied. "But I figured on finding a place here in Greenport."

Water sluiced over the sides of the coffee maker as Joy poured from the pot. Of course he wanted to stay in Greenport! All the better to see Diana.

"There's no need for you to look for someplace to stay. There's certainly plenty of room here," Emily Mackey announced. "The downstairs is a mess with all the painting going on, but the bedrooms are all fine."

"That would be great, but are you sure I won't be in the way?"

Joy gnawed her bottom lip as she mopped up water from the counter with a sponge. Didn't anyone else realize what was going on here? Was she the only one that wasn't naive?

"Not another word about it," Emily Mackey insisted. "Joy, I'll finish making the coffee. Would you two girls go up and get a room ready? Nick, please finish your sandwich. I've got cherry pie for you. I baked just this morning.''

Joy and Diana left the kitchen. Kevin walked out behind them to hang his coat and Diana's in the front hall closet. The three maneuvered around furniture that had been covered with heavy drop cloths and pushed into the middle of the living room. The front entryway was the only completed section on the first floor.

"Hurry up you two," Kevin said as Diana and Joy started up the stairs to the landing. "I can't stay too late. I've got briefs to go over tonight.''

"You'd better not be thinking of bringing any briefs on our honeymoon," Diana replied over her shoulder.

"I'm not figuring on bringing any *briefs* at all," Kevin called back up to Diana.

Diana smiled to Joy showing her amusement with Kevin's retort.

She wasn't in a smiling mood, but Joy gave it her all to smile back as they reached the second floor. "Did you ever think of not waiting any longer and just eloping?''

"Don't be silly," Diana answered with indignation. "I want a church wedding with all the trimmings. And I want my reception here, where no one else has had their reception. It's going to be just perfect having it here once everything's all together. Don't you think so?''

Joy wistfully nodded her head as she opened the door to the linen closet in the hallway. If she were getting married she'd want it to be just the way Diana had it planned.

"Which bedroom do you think we should put Nick in?" Diana asked her.

"How about the attic bedroom?" Joy suggested, gathering together a set of sheets.

"I think Mom would rather have us all on the same floor. Let's put him in the bedroom between yours and mine."

Joy scowled.

"What?" Diana asked.

"Nothing."

Diana wouldn't let it go. "Was it obvious to you, too?"

"Was what obvious?" Joy asked innocently.

"Nick. He's still in love with me. Did you see the look in his eyes when we said hello to each other?"

"I saw it."

"Poor Nick." Diana released a deep breath. "I really feel badly about it."

Joy didn't think Diana felt half as bad as *she* did—not that Joy imagined Nick could ever be interested in her, even if Diana was out of the picture.

Chapter Two

Nick couldn't sleep. He turned the lamp on next to his bed and reached for his watch. Seeing that it was nearing midnight, he realized he'd been tossing around for close to an hour. Could it have something to do with the pizza he'd shared with Joy at ten o'clock? They'd been the only two interested in food, so Nick had gone out and brought a pizza back. However, Nick decided his inability to sleep had less to do with the food he'd eaten and more to do with the company he'd shared it with.

Nick grinned and thought about Joy fast asleep and curled up in her bed. He wondered if she slept on her stomach. Or flat on her back the way she'd been on the pile of leaves. Flat on her back brought a red-hot image to his mind.

Slow it down, Tremain! How long ago was it—fleeting though it may have been—that you thought you were in love with Diana?

Knowing these thoughts would not help him sleep, he decided to go downstairs. He used the miniature pocket flashlight hanging from his key chain to find his way to the kitchen. Once in the cozy room he poured himself a glass of soda. His flashlight began blinking and he turned it off to conserve the battery. He drank his soda in the dark, something he'd often done out of occupational necessity.

Suddenly the kitchen was flooded with light. A surprised Nick was confronted with a bleary-eyed Joy, dressed in colorful flannel pajamas.

"What are you doing?" Joy asked as soon as she got over being startled at finding a very bare-chested man in her kitchen.

"I was thirsty." Nick held out his glass of soda. "What brought you downstairs?"

"Thirsty...very thirsty." She wasn't making any move to do anything about it. The muscles of his chest and forearms had her mesmerized.

"Must have been the pizza." Nick grinned.

"Uh-huh." *Uh-huh,* she thought...*uh-huh?* Is that all you can think to say? *Uh-huh!* You're a writer! You're supposed to be good with words.

"How about some cola?" Nick asked.

"Okay," Joy answered.

Nick put his glass on the counter and poured her drink. He held out the glass, and Joy felt as if she were walking in a dream as she came up to him. The coldness of the glass in her hand came as something of a shock. She wasn't conscious of having even accepted it.

"Love your pajamas." He gave her a full-wattage grin as she held the glass to her lips.

Joy gulped and sputtered. She looked down at herself after wiping her mouth with the back of her hand. She would hardly have picked to wear what she was wearing if she was conjuring this up as a dream.

"They were a present." Joy ran the tip of her tongue across her lips.

Nick dragged his eyes off her mouth and studied the array of small iridescent red hearts against the background of cream-colored flannel. "Did some guy give them to you?"

He knew she wasn't seriously involved with anyone. He knew because he'd asked Kevin. Indirectly, of course.

Joy shook her head. "A friend from work gave them to me for my birthday."

He liked that answer. "And when was your birthday?"

"February fourteenth, Valentine's Day."

"Cupid's baby, huh?" Nick grinned.

Joy nodded. Looking at his bare chest was causing her heart to flutter.

His eyes moved over her face. "Your chin looks a little sticky."

"Cola," Joy said.

Nick took hold of the hand she started to raise and kept it down at her side. He brought his free hand up and touched the damp spot on her chin.

Joy's lips parted. She was breathing haltingly through her mouth as his hand lifted her chin higher.

And then the kitchen door swung open.

"What are the two of you doing?" Diana asked, clothed in one of her seductive nightgowns. The thin, pink silk just missed being see-through.

"Drinking," Nick muttered, bringing his hand back down.

"We were both thirsty," Joy added. "And I had cola on my chin."

Diana proceeded to the refrigerator for the platter of cold chicken. "It isn't any wonder that you'd be thirsty. How the two of you can eat the food you eat is beyond me. Don't either of you have any concern for your bodies?"

Nick groaned to himself. He had a very definite interest in one of the bodies in the room. It wasn't his. Nor was it Diana's.

"Well," Joy said awkwardly. "I guess I've had enough. See you both in the morning."

"I've had enough, too," Nick said. "I'll walk up with you."

She looked over at him just once, as they walked toward the stairs. Had he been about to kiss her when Diana had walked in on them? No, Joy answered herself. So what had he been doing?

"Are you tired?" Nick asked as they reached Joy's bedroom door.

"Uh-huh," Joy answered, then moaned under her breath. "Aren't you?"

"Not really. But I guess since you're tired I won't try to persuade you to stay up with me a little longer."

Joy took a deep breath. Persuade! She was like putty in his hands.

"Well, see you tomorrow," Nick said with a smile.

"Tomorrow is a workday for me." Joy made herself open her bedroom door. "I leave early."

"I'm a pretty early riser myself."

"Even without much sleep?"

"Even without much sleep."

"Good night," she said.

"Good night," he answered.

Joy took a resolute step into her bedroom. Not looking back, she closed the door.

Nick stood in the hallway a second longer, wondering again what position she slept in.

Her mother was flipping pancakes as Joy came into the kitchen the next morning. After noting that no one else was in the room, Joy marched straight for the coffee that was already brewed.

Emily slipped a pancake onto a plate. "How many will you have? Two or three?"

"I don't have time for more than a swallow of coffee," Joy said to her mother. "I've overslept as it is." She hadn't fallen asleep until the wee hours of the morning. "Put them in the oven for Diana and Nick."

"If Diana eats half a pancake that will be a lot, and Nick has already eaten and left."

Joy put down the cup of coffee that she hadn't yet taken a swallow from. "Nick ate and left already? Where did he go?"

"He didn't say, dear." Emily looked at her youngest child thoughtfully. "I must say he didn't appear any less tired than you do this morning."

"I guess we were both attacked by pepperoni pizza." Joy gave her mother a kiss on the cheek, then hurried off.

* * *

The newsroom of the *Greenport News* was buzzing when Joy arrived. It was never a quiet place to begin with, but this morning there was an unusually high-pitched quality to the chatter.

Joy hung up her green reefer coat and glanced around. Even Arthur Dailey was in animated conversation with Bill Kellman. That was unusual. The two pressmen, both gray-haired, though Arthur had more on his pate than Bill, hardly ever spoke to each other. There was something about one having slighted the other sometime back. Way back. Joy suspected that neither man recalled the exact slight, nor which one of them had delivered it, or even exactly when it had happened.

"What's going on?" Joy asked, catching the ear of Pamela Cousins, a breezy forty-year-old blonde with an ample shape and a Ms. Congeniality personality. She manned the phone for the classifieds. There wasn't anyone who didn't like Pamela. Nor was there anyone who Pamela didn't like back.

"You know. The big news," Pamela said, turning from Cal Peterson who reported weekly on the activities of the Greenport wharf.

"What big news?" Joy asked.

"Oh," Pamela said. "I thought that was the reason you dressed up today. You know... to make an impression on *him*."

"'Him'?" The only *him* she'd wanted to make an impression on in her short, slim, gray wool skirt; clingy, white, ribbed-jersey turtleneck; high-heeled black pumps; and black panty hose had left before she'd come down to the kitchen. "What 'him'?"

"Our new boss. The man Earl sold the paper to."

"Earl sold the paper?" Joy was amazed.

"The new owner is in his office right now. Earl said he'll be introducing us all once you'd arrived. They've been waiting for you."

"I'll go tell Earl you're here," Cal said, breaking away.

"Have you seen the new owner?" Joy inquired of Pamela.

Pamela expressed her response to Joy's question with a big smile before she said, "God, I wish I was ten years younger and not married. The man is a S-T-U-D."

Earl Lansing came out of his office and into the main section of the news area with Cal Peterson and the man Pamela had just labeled a stud. Joy's mouth fell open. The stud at Earl Lansing's side was Nick Tremain.

Earl Lansing's eyes singled out Joy. "I assume you know by now?"

Joy got her mouth closed in time to nod her head. Her eyes flashed to Nick. He gave her a fast wink, then a very slow perusal. When his eyes did cruise back up to hers, there was sexy masculine approval in his gaze.

Joy felt her face get warm.

Nick grinned.

By then everyone in the office had gathered around.

"I am not going to give a speech," Earl began, looking delighted. "I'm sure you're all tired of hearing me complain about still working at my age—"

Cal Peterson cut in jokingly. "It's not fair of you to walk out without letting one of us win the yearly bet. Just how old are you?"

Earl chuckled. "Old enough to know better, but not old enough to stop doing it."

There was laughter and cheers.

Earl waved both his hands to bring the group to order. "Ladies and gentlemen ... may I present Nick Tremain, the new owner of the *Greenport News*. You've got a renowned photojournalist for a boss now, but I'll let him tell you about that himself."

Earl smiled at Nick. "It's all yours."

But it wasn't all Nick's yet, as the staff crowded around Earl to wish him well. In that moment only Joy stood to one side, where Nick's full attention was on her. There was a hint of devilishness around his mouth. Joy flicked him a look of sheer incredulity before she included herself among Earl's well-wishers.

"I'm not leaving without a big hug from you," Earl smiled, getting to Joy last.

"Oh, Earl," Joy said emotionally as the hug ended. "I'm really going to miss you." She'd already had that feeling on her mind, knowing she was going to give three weeks' notice this morning.

Earl fondly patted Joy's shoulder as he looked out at all the people who had worked for him. "Is tomorrow enough time for you to get a cake for me?"

Pamela called out, "I'm going to bake you my triple-layer chocolate cake."

Someone joked, "Is that the one we have to use a saw on?"

Earl smiled broadly. "Settle down, kiddies. And behave yourselves."

Cal Peterson said, "So you finally get to take your wife to Florida. Pearl must be dancing a jig."

"She's certainly nagged me about it long enough," Earl replied. "But I will be around a few more days just to make sure you all stay in line. Only right now I'm going out to have myself a long, leisurely breakfast while the man of the hour takes over." Earl gave Nick a two-finger salute.

A tense silence filled the newsroom as soon as Earl walked out. All eyes were on Nick. Joy was certain she was the only one that noticed Nick was a little tense himself. She could tell just from the way he stood.

Nick smiled at the group. "Let me begin by saying that my intention is to be more than an editor. I'm planning to work out in the field, as well."

The twenty-eight-year-old staff photographer for the *Greenport News* cleared his throat. "I'm real familiar with your photos, Mr. Tremain. I guess you won't be needing me around here anymore."

"You're George DeGeneris, right?" Nick questioned.

"Yes, sir." George put an uneasy hand up to his hair in a reflexive motion, but the untamable blond cowlick sprang right back up.

"Cut the 'sir.'" Nick grinned. "Now it may take me a little time to put a name to all your faces, but I am fully aware of the work each and every one of you do around here. And I haven't seen anything to complain about. I'm especially familiar with your photos, George. Your concepts are fresh and alive. What I'm going to want is more of the same. A lot more of the same. I want a lot more of the same from all of you, but I'm also going to want you to stretch beyond where you've been. We're going to create something together. Something new and different.

"We are not going to be just a local paper anymore. We're going to feature stories that today's top magazines will envy. We're not going to just deliver the news. We're going to tell the stories behind the news. In-depth stories about the people that make the news and not just in Greenport. We're going to cover the entire East End. We are going to become the *East End Journal* and we are going to give the 'big boys' a run for the money. And, by the way, it's Nick and not Mr. Tremain."

The applause came. It started slowly then built up. And the ice was broken, replaced by an excitement that permeated the room.

Joy saw Nick take a deep breath and then give one of his easy, relaxed smiles. She felt the same exhilaration as her co-workers and thought about how much she would have liked to be a part of his plans.

Nick made a kidding motion with a slice of his hand in front of his throat to quiet the buzz that had started. Succeeding, he spoke again. "I'm going to want to meet personally with each one of you throughout the day. Right now I think we all need another cup of coffee."

Except for Joy and Nick, the staff dispersed to queue up in front of the coffee maker.

"How about being the first one I meet with personally?" Nick asked with a teasing grin that was meant only for her.

Joy wanted to return his dynamite smile, but she didn't. "Actually there is something I need to speak to you about," she replied in a professional tone.

The smile left Nick's mouth as his eyes searched hers. He nodded briefly and then led the way to the office that had just become his.

"Sit down," Nick said, once they'd both entered the room and he'd closed the door—and after they'd stood for a fraction of a second just evaluating each other. She was nervous. He could read that easily, though she was working at not letting it show.

Joy settled herself into one of the two wooden chairs in front of the desk while Nick took the chair behind the desk. He leaned forward.

Joy swallowed. "I can't believe you've bought the paper. But, anyway, everyone loved your ideas."

"Did you?" He was studying her closely.

"Absolutely." Her eyes became bright with the excitement he'd engendered with his comments before Joy dropped them to look at her lap.

Nick watched her pull the hem of her skirt down some. It still didn't get any nearer to her knees.

Joy swallowed again. "I was going to give Earl three weeks' notice this morning. It seems that you're the one that I'm going to have to give my notice to now." There was no way she could stay and work with him, not feeling the way she did about him. Just thinking about it was torture.

Nick felt like he'd just had his lights punched out. He picked up a pen from the desk and fiddled with it. How was he supposed to court her with her taking off? "You have three more months to run on your contract here."

"I know that." Joy's focus was on the pen he was holding, not his eyes.

"Would you mind telling me what brought you to this decision?"

"I've been offered an assignment with *New World* magazine. They're going to be sending reporters out to a number of South American countries to do stories on daily life. I'm slated to go to Bolivia. There's still some reservation on their part, but they're giving me a shot." It was her chance to, if nothing else, have a stimulating career for herself.

"There shouldn't be any reservations on their part. They don't deserve you if they haven't figured out how talented you are."

Joy's gray-green eyes came up to find sincerity written on his face. She felt all aglow at his praise.

This time it was Nick who broke eye contact. "I'm not letting you out of your contract."

Joy blinked. "That's ridiculous. In three weeks' time you'll find a hundred reporters to take my place."

"I want you," Nick said tersely, his eyes back on her.

"I can't stay, Nick," Joy said just as succinctly while their gazes locked.

Nick dropped the pen to the desk. "I don't see that you have any choice but to work out your contract. I am not accepting your notice."

"I have a choice. I can break my contract," Joy returned rigidly.

"Try it and I'll sue you," Nick said, bluffing.

Joy tipped up her unsteady chin. She didn't know if she wanted to cry or throw something at him. "You'd actually sue me?"

He didn't answer, just continued to look at her.

Joy no longer felt the threat of tears. What she felt was frustration and anger. "What made you decide to buy this paper, anyway?"

"I decided it was time for me to settle down in one place and build roots."

Joy thought about his answer for a long moment.

"I get it," she said, pushing back her chair and standing. Of course, she got it. He was showing Diana that he'd settled down. It was his traveling that had broken them up.

"What do you get?" Nick asked, reaching her as she got to the door.

Joy turned around to give him a withering glance. "We both know why you picked now to settle down."

Nick couldn't hold back a grin. She looked so cute with her eyes blazing at him. "I really don't think you have a clue."

"Oh, I have a clue. I have more than a clue," Joy retorted.

"Forget what you think you know." Nick put his palms to the door on either side of her, pinning her in place. "How about we talk about a compromise?"

"What kind of compromise?" Joy asked, partly steaming, partly intoxicated by his proximity. More intoxicated than steaming. And thrilled. Being praised by someone of his professional stature was exhilarating.

"You work out the rest of your contract without being angry at me, and if you still want to leave then I'll see that you get an assignment from someone who will appreciate you. It's obvious you haven't met with the right people."

Joy narrowed her eyes at him. "Is this a snow job?"
Even if it was, Joy realized, what choice did she have?
She couldn't imagine any editor hiring a journalist
who had been sued for breach of contract.

"No."

"Can I go to my desk now?" How in heaven's name
was she going to get through three months of being
around him?

"Are you still mad at me?" Nick angled his head.

"Yes." She didn't get all that much conviction in
her tone. It was impossible for her to disassociate herself from his sexiness.

"How about if I buy you pizza with anchovies for
lunch?" Nick asked lazily.

"Are you planning to eat at the same table?" Remembering how he had balked the night before about
her topping choice Joy did her utmost to keep a
straight face. His playfulness was irresistible.

"Is that a smile you're trying to hide?"

"No!" Joy pushed firmly at his shoulders.

Nick easily maintained his position. "Are you going to have lunch with me?"

"Anchovies?" Joy asked.

"Anchovies," Nick responded with a laugh.

"And you have to taste a slice."

"Okay." Nick put his hands up in the air as if she
was holding a gun on him. "You've got me at your
mercy."

Joy let him see her smile as she made a backward
reach for the doorknob. There wasn't any way that she
could stay mad at him.

"God, you really are hard on a guy," Nick said with
a grin and stepped back to let her go.

Chapter Three

"What have you been up to all day?" Diana asked, addressing Nick as soon as he and Joy stepped into the parlor that evening.

"I've been running a newspaper." Nick winked at Joy. "Trying to, anyway. I might have done better if your sister hadn't forced me to eat anchovies at lunch."

Joy's smile was forced. She'd been happily keyed up since they'd had lunch together, but now that he was about to tell Diana that he'd finally settled down, Joy's spirits flattened right out.

"A newspaper?" Diana questioned, confused.

"The *East End Journal,*" Nick responded, giving a glance to the fourth party in the room. There was a young man standing on a stepladder closing a paint can. Nick didn't think Joy was picking up on it, but the painter was giving her a thorough once-over. Every fiber of Nick's body went on alert.

"Formerly the *Greenport News*," Joy said.

"I don't get it," Diana said, as the painter got down from the ladder.

"Hey, Joy," he said, flashing her a look—a look that Nick was clearly reading as predatory. He wasn't liking this one bit!

"Hey, yourself, Eddie," Joy said while Nick watched her smile at the painter. To Nick that smile seemed to have come to her easier than the smile she'd given him moments ago.

"I still don't get it," Diana said again.

"I haven't seen you dress this way for a day at the slave den before," Eddie said, giving Joy a provokingly sexy grin, then a low whistle.

Nick ground his teeth almost to the point of needing emergency dental treatment.

"Yeah...well," was Joy's lackadaisical response while she tried not comparing herself to Diana. Even in humdrum textured slacks and a plain white shirt rolled to her elbows, Diana was a knockout. Joy wouldn't have traded Diana for any other sister in the entire world. But the three inches of height Diana had over her was aggravating Joy right now. Couldn't Diana have at least one shortcoming?

Forcing her thoughts away from her sister, Joy asked Eddie. "How's the rock and roll business?"

"Happening, babe. Happening."

Nick watched "Mr. Happening" drop his eyes to briefly explore, for a second time, the fit of Joy's turtleneck top across her pert breasts.

Joy finally turned to Nick. "Oh, Nick...this is Eddie DeMarco. Painter by day. Rock and roll singer by night. Eddie, this is Nick Tremain. My new boss and Kevin's brother."

"Your new boss?" Diana asked, still bewildered.

Eddie raised a paint-covered palm toward Nick's face. "I'd shake hands with you, but—"

"No problem." Nick ground out a casual smile, taking adversarial note of Eddie DeMarco's cocky physical characteristics. What did Joy know of Eddie DeMarco's nights? Did she go for guys with pony-tails?

"Will someone please answer me?" Diana looked from Nick to Joy, then back to Nick.

Just then Emily Mackey pushed open the door from the kitchen. "Dinner is ready. Hurry up. All of you. There's nothing worse than a lukewarm roast. Eddie, haven't you changed and washed up yet?"

"I'm going right now, 'Mom,'" Eddie bantered.

"I'm just going to change my clothes," Joy said.

"Need any help?" Eddie teased Joy as Mrs. Mackey stepped back into the kitchen.

"No, thanks," Joy answered sassily.

Eddie's advances toward Joy had Nick steaming as he started out behind the two of them. Nick got to the front hall and was about to go upstairs to change out of his suit when Diana waylaid him.

"Nick Tremain, you tell me what is going on." Diana placed her hands firmly on Nick's shoulders after moving in front of him.

"I bought the *Greenport News*," Nick answered distractedly, his blue eyes following Joy as she went up the stairs with Eddie DeMarco at her side. Nick could tell Eddie was saying something to her, but he couldn't hear what it was. Whatever it was, it brought another smile to Joy's lips. Nick ground his teeth again.

"You bought Joy's newspaper!" Diana exclaimed. "Does that mean you've given up being a vagabond?"

Nick inattentively nodded his head while he continued eyeing Eddie and Joy. He'd been congratulating himself since this morning at getting her to stay at the paper. He hadn't factored in any romantic competition into the picture.

"This is going to be good for you, Nick. I just know it is." Diana looped her arms around Nick's neck to give him a hug.

It was that embrace that Joy saw as she turned at the top of the stairs and glanced over the railing.

"See you in five," Eddie said.

Joy forced her eyes off Diana and Nick down below and waved distractedly to Eddie. Heavyhearted, Joy walked to her bedroom.

"Have you told Kevin?" Diana asked as Nick released himself from her embrace.

"Not yet," Nick answered, doing some more wrestling with his stupidity. Hell, it wasn't like Joy had given him any sign of interest since he'd returned.

"Kevin is going to be very relieved," Diana was saying. "He worries a lot about his baby brother."

"I worry about him. It's been just the two of us for years now." Nick didn't allow himself to dwell on the car accident that had robbed them of their parents eight years ago. Instead, he pushed as he always did to remember the rich, full happy life his parents had enjoyed together. It was that kind of happy marriage he wanted one day for himself.

"You don't have to worry about Kevin," Diana said. "You'd better hurry up and change if you're changing. Mom does hate serving a roast lukewarm."

Nick started for the stairs, then stopped and turned back. His hand came down from the tie he'd just started to loosen. "Does Eddie DeMarco have dinner here often?"

"Pretty often. Mom's sort of adopted him since he's been working here. I've been using him for over a year now with all my clients. He's got a truly artistic eye for color. I've never seen anyone paint the way he paints. He just about makes love to the wall."

Nick gave the knot of his tie a further pull. "Has he got something going with Joy?"

"Do you mean are they involved?" Diana made a twirling motion with one hand.

Nick nodded his head tightly.

"Joy's gone out with him. He is great looking, but it's hard to tell with Joy. Since the guy she went with in college she hasn't dated anyone more than three times. If I'm counting correctly, Eddie's had his allotment."

"Is she carrying a torch for the guy she went with in college?" Nick disquietingly picked out what seemed to be the most salient point.

"If Joy's still in love with Paul Reeves, she'd tell me. We tell each other everything," Diana answered. "Now, you'd better hurry up if you're going to change."

Up in her bedroom Joy replaced her panty hose with white athletic socks and her skirt with a pair of body-hugging jeans. And she'd left her clingy white-ribbed turtleneck on.

Joy glowered at herself in a full-length mirror after tying her sneakers.

"Idiot!" she scolded her reflection. She'd already shown off her meager attributes to Nick all day long. Diana beat her out there, too, by inches.

Though she'd had a head start, Nick was already in the kitchen when Joy came through the door. She was the last one down. Eddie was kiddingly pestering her mother by making faces into a steamer pot of broccoli. He'd changed from his painting clothes to clean jeans and a T-shirt under a tan flannel shirt that he'd left hanging out and unbuttoned.

Joy's eyes skidded past Eddie to Nick as he stood involved in a conversation with Diana. He'd swapped his suit and dress shoes for jeans, a navy pullover sweater and boots. He looked loose, casually hip and incredibly sexy. He was sexy no matter what he wore. Or didn't wear—like last night in the kitchen when he'd been lethally nude from the waist up.

Joy's mind went to dreamland, where having Nick fall in love with her was wholly achievable. She even added a few inches to her measurements while she was at it.

"You've got enough to deal with right now," Nick was saying to Diana, while meeting Joy's gaze for a fraction of a second before she turned her head away. He'd been aware of her the instant she'd walked into the room.

"If I concentrate any more on the wedding, I'm going to make myself crazy," Diana responded. "Let me scout for you. I know your taste."

Emily Mackey put the roast on a platter. "Everyone to the table."

Eddie was already seated and waiting.

"Let me get that," Nick said, moving from Diana to lift the roast off the counter. "I can't say I haven't yearned for home cooking, but I wish you hadn't fussed. My staying here is making extra work for you."

Joy took in the truly appreciative look on Nick's face. It was the sweetest look she'd ever seen on a guy.

"I am not fussing. I love having a houseful." Emily Mackey earnestly dismissed Nick's concern as she ladled the broccoli into a serving dish. "You could do something for me, though. You could do the carving."

"Sure," Nick replied and brought the roast to the table while Joy spooned mashed potatoes from a pot to a bowl and Diana went to the refrigerator for the salad that was already cut up.

Standing, Nick began carving as Joy, Diana and Mrs. Mackey took their seats with all the fixings for dinner on the table.

"What are you going to scout around for?" Joy asked Diana.

"A house for Nick. One he can lease with an option to buy." Diana looked up at Nick. "Something modern, right?"

"No." Nick shook his head. "I'm not into modern at all."

"Something old and with character," Joy said, reflecting her own taste.

"Exactly," Nick responded with a smile. He was surprised, but not shocked that they thought alike.

"Do you have any plans for tonight?" Eddie asked Joy, bringing Nick out of his reverie.

"No," Joy answered listlessly.

"How about coming with me to Gillie's in West-hampton? I'm going to be singing there for a week starting tomorrow night."

"Well . . ."

"Come on," Eddie coaxed. "I could use your help checking out the acoustics."

Joy considered the evening ahead, being in the company of Nick and Diana as they talked about houses. "All right," Joy answered carelessly.

Nick clenched his jaw. *What had happened to her three strikes and you're out?*

With a white-knuckled grip on the carving knife, Nick hacked at the next slice of meat.

"I think we have enough meat to start with," Emily said to Nick.

"Do you have any plans for tonight?" Nick asked Diana as he took his seat. He wasn't about to be sty-mied.

"No." Diana shrugged one shoulder. "I don't get to see Kevin at all during the week."

"How about we join Joy and Eddie?" There was one thing Nick was sure about. Eddie DeMarco was all wrong for her.

Joy held her breath. God, he was smooth. Nick was going to have Diana dating him again with barely a crook of his finger. He had innocence down to a science.

Eddie made an unsuccessful attempt not to look vexed at being aced out of his plan to be alone with

Joy. Nick had no trouble at all noting Eddie's irritation.

"Sounds like fun," Diana replied.

Joy turned to her mother. "Mom, how about coming along?"

"I have my evening all planned out. There's a movie on TV that I want to see. Besides, I don't go to places named Gillie's. You all go along and have fun."

Fun? Joy thought. Not likely.

The music was blasting as they entered Gillie's, compliments of a platinum blond female singer with a tinny voice, accompanied by a bass player, synthesizer and guitarist. Nick couldn't imagine acoustics being any concern. Gillie's took up no more than two small storefronts in the strip center where it was located. Then again, Nick didn't think for one minute that acoustics had been on Eddie's mind when he'd asked Joy out for the night.

They walked to an area of tables set around a stamp-sized dance floor where a few couples grooved to the beat. Almost all of the tables were empty. The action was at the bar, which took up most of the space.

After everyone had removed their coats Eddie grabbed Joy's hand before any of them could sit. "Come on, let's dance."

"Diana?" Nick invited, instantaneously choosing between sitting at the table watching Joy dance with Eddie from a distance or watching her with Eddie DeMarco at close range. He was rankled either way.

Diana's eyes lit up. "I'd love to dance."

Nick fit Diana conservatively in his arms. Over Diana's shoulder, Nick's eyes went to Joy and Eddie.

There was nothing at all conservative in the way Eddie was maneuvering to hold Joy. Nick saw Joy place a firm hand against Eddie's chest, staving him off, claiming space for herself. And with that Nick breathed easier.

"It's funny how things work out," Diana said, smiling philosophically with her head tipped back to look up at him. "You buy the *Greenport News*, and I wind up engaged to Kevin."

"Who would have thought it," Nick said inconsequentially, finding it easy enough to lead Diana to the music, though his attention was focused on Joy and Eddie.

"You can take your hand off my chest." Eddie gave Joy an exasperated look. "I won't pull you any closer if you don't want me to. I do understand that some women need a lot more time than others. Right?"

"Right." Joy presented a quickly fading smile. She did bring the hand in question up from his chest to his shoulder. But she kept her elbow at the ready.

Eddie squeezed Joy's other hand—the one he had pinned down at her side. "What's the story with Nick Tremain?"

"What do you mean?" Joy felt Eddie slide the hand he'd had between her shoulder blades just a bit lower.

"Is there something more between the two of you than employer and employee?" Eddie's hand moved another small inch down Joy's back.

Joy sucked in her breath. "He's my boss and his brother is going to marry my sister. That's all there is between us."

Eddie's hand progressed another inch down Joy's spine. "Call it a vibe but I think he's interested in you. And I don't mean just as an employee or friend."

Joy nearly laughed. "You don't know how ridiculous that is."

"How ridiculous is it?"

"He's in love with someone else." Joy went from almost laughing to wanting to cry.

"Someone you know?"

"Yes," Joy answered miserably.

"Diana?"

Joy's eyes popped. "What made you say Diana?"

"She told me this afternoon about Kevin's brother showing up and that she'd been engaged to him." Eddie's roving hand got closer to the small of her back.

Joy neither denied nor confirmed Eddie's speculation. She let it hang. Just then Joy caught Nick's eyes glancing her way, and because he happened to be looking, Joy gave Eddie her flirtiest smile. She wanted Nick to know that there were men who found her attractive. Not that there was any point to his knowing.

Eddie smiled back seductively. "Bet he's the type to try and get Diana jealous by coming on to you. She goes for his brother. He goes for her sister. Maybe that's the vibe I'm getting."

"He is not going to do anything of the sort." Joy rousingly admonished Eddie's sophomoric attitude. "He'd never stoop to trying to make Diana jealous with me. Could you bring your hand up a little?" Joy requested in a firm, determined voice as Eddie's fingers began to spread intimately below her spine.

"I don't get it, Joy," Eddie grumbled, bringing his hand up. "You've been giving me signals."

Joy guiltily considered Eddie's remark. He was absolutely right. She had given him signals. "Didn't you say yourself that some women need more time?"

Eddie issued a groan. "Is there any chance of anything happening between us in this lifetime?"

Joy gave Eddie a conciliatory "Mona Lisa" smile, which made her feel even more guilty. Playing the game she was playing wasn't like her. Testily, Joy placed the blame on Nick.

"Most women find me very sexy." Eddie quirked a sexy corner-of-the-mouth smile. "Especially when I'm on stage singing. I had a woman throw me a pair of panties once. It happens to Mick all the time. I couldn't believe it was happening to me."

"Mick?" Joy inquired, doing her damnedest to make it seem like she was impressed.

"Jagger... Rolling Stones. He's my idol."

"Right. Jagger."

"Are you going to come and hear me sing?"

"Sure," Joy answered. "I'll get a whole group together."

"How about coming alone? I'm on a real high after I sing."

Joy's gaze collided again with Nick's. "I'll have to think about it," she said, guiltily working another superficially vampy smile on Eddie.

"Kevin is going to be wearing a monkey suit and so are you," Diana insisted. "You are going to be part of the wedding party now that you're here, even though Kevin couldn't reach you in time to name you as his best man. He really did want you to be his best man.

It would have been great with Joy as my maid of honor and you as Kevin's best man.''

"Who is Kevin's best man?" Nick was sorry he wasn't standing up for his brother. Who was going to be escorting Joy? Had Diana invited Eddie DeMarco to the wedding?

"Rick Farrell. You know Kevin's partner, don't you?"

"Yes. Kevin and Rick go all the way back to law school. I remember Kevin being Rick's best man when Rick got married a few years ago."

"Rick is divorced now. I'm hoping that Rick and Joy hit it off. I can see Joy with Rick. He's got a sharp mind. He's lots of fun and he's very nice-looking."

"I can't see Joy with Rick," Nick said, doubly frustrated now. "He's too old for her."

"Eleven years is not necessarily that much of a spread. I know it won't bother Joy. Anyway, I've added another bridesmaid just for you. Rachel Harmon. She's Joy's best friend. Joy and I have mostly the same friends."

Diana's voice went up a notch. "I just realized I haven't told Joy yet that I added Rachel to the wedding party this morning. I was worried that Rachel would be put off that I was asking her to be a bridesmaid at the last moment, but she was fine about it. You're going to like Rachel. I told her all about you."

"Forget it! I don't want to be matched up."

"Snap out of it, Nick," Diana said ruefully.

"Snap out of what?" Nick's frustration peaked. "I've had this conversation with Kevin. I'm fine about the two of you."

"I'm glad you're fine about us," Diana replied placatingly, though she didn't look convinced. "Are Joy and Eddie still dancing?"

"They're still dancing," Nick answered tautly, as Diana craned her neck to look for herself. Seeing Joy smile at Eddie again, Nick became even more tense than he already was. He wasn't consciously aware of himself counting, but that had to have been the sixth time she'd smiled at Eddie.

"I think Joy may be more interested in Eddie than she's been letting on to me," Diana commented.

Nick told himself that if Eddie had been *at all* right for Joy, he'd stop chasing her himself. But Eddie wasn't at all right for her.

Nick gave a brief thought to letting his hair grow long enough for a ponytail.

"I don't believe it!" Diana said. "Kevin just came in. He's looking for us." Diana and Nick stopped dancing to wave to Kevin.

Seeing Diana and Nick waving to Kevin, Joy stopped in her tracks, bringing Eddie to a halt.

"I called the house," Kevin said, approaching both couples. "Your mother told me where you'd gone."

Diana moved from Nick to Kevin. "Did you finish your work?"

"Enough to get me by in court tomorrow." Kevin put his arm possessively around Diana's shoulders. "I got off the phone with your mother and I was sitting there thinking of you being out with this brother of mine." Kevin raised an eyebrow at Nick.

Nick put his hands up and smiled. "I've been a perfect gentlemen. You can ask Joy."

Joy's gaze darted to Nick. If he was at all bothered by Kevin showing up, he wasn't revealing it. Sure, he'd been acting proper with Diana since they'd gotten here. But what about the drive over? They'd come in two cars. Nick had insisted on driving. Eddie had insisted on driving. Diana had mediated them into two cars.

"I'll ask Diana, thank you," Kevin rejoined.

Diana laughed. "Wait till I tell you what this brother of yours has been up to. And I don't mean with me."

"Hey, Eddie." Gilbert Benson, the forty-nine-year-old, balding proprietor of Gillie's, called to him from behind the bar. "Come here a minute."

"Be right back," Eddie said, speeding off at the summons.

"Can I get you to dance with me?" Diana turned coquettish eyes up at Kevin.

"I've promised to dance with you at our wedding." Kevin smiled lovingly. "Can I get you to sit down with me?"

"Well," Diana joshed. "Since you've promised in the presence of witnesses, I guess you can get me to sit."

Nick gave some coins in his pocket a restless jingle as he looked at Joy. "What do you say we give these soon-to-be-married folks a little time to themselves? How about dancing with me?"

Joy's stomach immediately lurched, while her heart began pounding against her ribs. His question had stopped her from following Diana and Kevin as they started for the table.

"Well ... I ... ah ..." Joy stammered.

Nick held on to Joy's gaze with his eyes. "You can't put a man through what I went through at lunch, then refuse to dance with him."

"The anchovies?" Joy asked dumbly, doing what she could to catch her breath. He was giving her the sexiest smile imaginable.

"Damn right! The anchovies." Nick put his arms around her and brought his body closer to hers, then waited for her to acquiesce.

With her heartbeat driving hard and fast at her throat, Joy brought a hand up to dangle tentatively around his neck. He joined his fingers lightly at the hollow of her spine. Joy placed her other hand on his shoulder. His head dropped down. Hers lifted up.

Keep it slow, Nick mentally telegraphed to the blond singer on the platform.

Don't let him know how I feel, Joy silently begged, making herself as stiff as she could.

"Did I tell you how much I like the suggestion you gave me to do a series on the new East End economics?" Joy asked in a nervously rapid speech while he started swaying with the sensuous beat of the music. *Were their feet moving?* Or was it just their bodies? A whole series of heated fantasies were flashing in her head, all of them with Nick Tremain in the leading role, in varying stages of undress.

"I only came up with the suggestion from something you said. That makes it all your idea," Nick murmured.

"No. It was your idea." The shoulder of his sweater was wonderfully soft against her chin. "I don't even remember what I said to give you the thought." Her fingers were close to his hair. She wanted to touch.

Just one quick touch. Could she do it without him knowing?

"You were talking about wineries—that started the ball rolling. I just gave your idea a broad stroke. It wouldn't be anything without your punchy title... 'Secrets of the new East End economics—people and families.' I love it."

Joy felt Nick's lips brush up against her cheek. She was certain it was accidental, but in the state he already had her in, it was more than enough to make the small steps she was taking go all haywire. Her foot tangled with his. She had to clutch his shoulder with the hand that was already there and grip his neck with the crook of her arm so as not to lose her balance. For half a second he teetered with her before steadying both of them.

"Okay now?" Nick asked gently, pulling his head back to see her face. He studied the pink, flustered cheeks and the way her eyes self-consciously cast about for someplace to center on other than him.

Joy could have died on the spot. She was that embarrassed. "It's hard for me to dance this way," she said, trying to mitigate her klutziness. She'd never tripped over herself this way before.

Nick reached up for the hand behind his neck and changed their position to a more conventional dance pose. From the corner of his eye, Nick saw Eddie leave the bar and head over to them. Was Eddie the reason she'd suddenly protested about the way they'd been dancing?

Joy concentrated her gaze on their meshed hands, wondering if he could feel the riotous jumping of her heart all the way through her fingers.

"You're not going to believe this," Eddie said, his voice startling Joy, causing her to nearly trip again before Nick stopped them entirely.

"Gillie asked me to help him out behind the bar tonight," Eddie said to Joy. "One of his bartenders didn't show. I tried saying no, but you know how it is. Gillie's acting like he's about to change his mind about giving me and the boys this gig. I'll be done by one, one-thirty at the latest, and then I'll take you home. You can sit at the bar and wait for me. I could shoot myself for letting Gillie know I've bartended before."

"Don't worry about Joy," Nick said, more than happy now that Diana had pushed them into two cars. "I'll drive her home. This way she can leave when she's ready to leave."

Eddie shot Nick a glare that didn't disturb Nick in the least.

"Hey, Eddie," Gillie yelled over. "Put a move on it."

"Come sit at the bar," Eddie coaxed Joy. "Keep me company."

"It looks like it's pretty rushed at the bar right now," Joy responded, much to Nick's delight.

"Eddie," Gillie paged again, even more impatiently.

Eddie put a hand up toward Gillie. "If I don't get to spend any more time with you tonight, I'll see you at the house tomorrow when you get home from work. By the way, I'm going to be around for a while. I don't know if Diana told you, but she'd asked me to paint all the bedrooms in the house after the wedding. Don't tell your Mom. Diana and Kevin want it to be a surprise."

Nick groaned under his breath, thinking of Eddie having a ready-made excuse to be around Joy even after the wedding.

"That's nice of Diana and Kevin, isn't it?" Joy smiled to Nick after Eddie hurried off.

"Real nice." Nick spoke through his teeth.

Joy looked toward the tables. "I guess we should go join Diana and Kevin."

Nick shook his head. "I didn't get a whole dance. You still owe me."

"I only made you eat one small taste of anchovies," Joy said impudently, but already turning into his arms before he changed his mind.

Nick put a testing hand out, palm upward to accept Joy's hand. It wasn't the way he wanted to dance with her.

Joy put her hand in his, letting her other hand fall limp at her side, deciding not to let her fingers anywhere near his hair again.

Nick started them both off in an unhurried rhythm.

"Oh, Nicky," Kevin razzed from the table. "The group just signed off for a break."

Joy blushed. She hadn't realized the music had stopped.

Nick raised his eyes to the ceiling. "Just what I need. A brother with a big mouth."

Chapter Four

"My brother the entrepreneur," Kevin said kiddingly to Nick, as he and Joy approached the table. "Why didn't you tell me you bought the newspaper?"

"I was trying to be dramatic," Nick said with a grin, seating Joy and then himself at the table. "I know better than to tell you anything I don't want broadcasted."

Kevin held a hand to his chest in mock pretense of being hurt. "I hope you had some lawyer look over the contract of sale before you signed it."

"Pay some lawyer the fee you lawyers get, when I have one in the family... Are you nuts? I put in a stipulation that my attorney had the right to negotiate any changes in the first week. The papers should be on your desk tomorrow morning. I mailed everything to you."

Kevin breathed a sigh of relief. "What made you decide on buying a newspaper now?"

Joy could have answered that. She knew Diana could have answered, as well.

"Your lectures finally worked on me," Nick said. "I'm settling down."

Kevin raised a salutatory thumb in the air. "I don't know what made you decide to settle down, but I'm certainly glad you have. Finally I get to stop worrying about you traipsing around with guerrillas somewhere or another."

"What's Eddie doing behind the bar?" Diana asked, looking very much like she wanted to change the topic of conversation.

"He's suffering the cost of fame," Nick answered offhandedly. "One of the bartenders didn't make it in and Eddie got recruited. Doesn't look like there's anyone waiting tables tonight, either. How about I go over to the bar and get us some drinks?"

"One round to celebrate your settling down," Kevin responded. "It's an hour to Greenport, then an hour back for me."

The evening, as far as Nick was concerned, had just made another turn for the better. Kevin deciding to drive Diana home had Nick ecstatic.

"It doesn't make any sense for you to spend two hours traveling back and forth. I'll go with Nick," Diana said. "Joy, are you going to wait for Eddie?"

"No," Joy replied. "I'm going home with Nick, also." Had he meant to sound as disappointed as he'd sounded when the band's break had ended their dancing? Joy berated herself for having the thought, much less for feeling hopeful.

"In that case," Kevin sent Diana a teasing smile. "I don't have any problem letting Nick take you home."

"You don't have a problem either way," Diana parried.

Joy examined Nick's face. He looked glum. Joy didn't have to think hard to figure out why. When he'd offered to take her off Eddie's hands, he hadn't thought he'd have another chance to be alone with Diana—not with Kevin having shown up.

"What would you ladies like to drink?" Nick asked, as he and Kevin got to their feet.

"What are you going to have?" Diana asked Kevin.

"White wine."

"That's good for me," Diana said.

"Joy?" Nick asked.

"Umm." Joy contemplated. "I think I'll have . . . a margarita." She was going for some dramatics herself.

Diana gaped at Joy. "A margarita? Since when do you drink anything hard? You barely even drink wine."

Joy gave a decided lift of her chin and then lied through her teeth. "I drink more than wine sometimes. I feel like having a margarita tonight."

Nick's bemused eyes were on Joy's upturned face. "It's a powerful drink," he said, with a grin in his voice at her expressive zealousness.

"I can handle it. I've had margaritas before." Joy punched up her lie with an air of sophistication that she centered on Nick. Who did he think he was? Patronizing her as if she was a kid. She was a woman! She could even roar if she wanted to.

"A margarita it is," Nick said, curbing his smile. Her eyes were telling him clearly that a smile wasn't the kind of response she wanted.

"I'm really concerned that Nick will try to do something to ruin the wedding," Diana said, after Nick and Kevin had left for the bar.

"I think Nick's mind is more on his plans for the paper than on your wedding." Joy could feel her heart in her throat. She liked that supposition, though she didn't honestly believe it.

"What I'd like to know is exactly when Nick decided to buy the paper." Diana cast her head to one side, tossing her pitch-black hair over one shoulder. "It's all very suspicious to me."

"Why don't you just ask him?" Now that Diana brought it up, Joy wondered about that herself. How had he even known that Earl was interested in selling? "Anyway, Kevin doesn't seem worried."

"Of course not. But you don't know Kevin the way I do. I know it's terrible of me, but I do like him trying not to show that he's concerned."

"That's a lousy game to play, Diana," Joy preached, dismissing her own guilty complicity at playing games with Eddie.

"You're being a pain, Joy." Diana wrinkled up her nose. "Oh, I almost forgot. I told Kevin, but I didn't tell you. I called Rachel this morning, and she's agreed to be another one of my bridesmaids. That evens things up again with Nick here. Wouldn't it be great if Nick took a liking to Rachel? What I should do is get them together before the wedding."

Joy felt as if her heart plunged to the pit of her stomach. Rachel Harmon was almost as beautiful as Diana.

"Eddie says to tell you he wants you to be sure to spend some time with him before you leave," Kevin told Joy as he and Nick arrived back at the table.

Thanks a lot, Kevin, Nick thought, scowling.

"Okay," Joy responded absently, looking down at the drink Nick placed before her.

Seated, Nick lifted his bottle of beer, offering a toast. "To settling down. To Joy being my ace reporter. To Diana and Kevin's upcoming wedding." *And to getting Eddie DeMarco out of the way.* Nick tacked on silently.

Diana and Kevin raised their wineglasses and clinked them together. Then they clinked separately to Nick's bottle of beer.

Joy picked up her margarita and joined the clinking.

His eyes on Joy, Nick took a swallow of his beer.

Diana and Kevin took sips of their wine.

Joy sampled the margarita first with the tip of her tongue. Finding the lime taste not at all unpleasant, and being thirsty, Joy swallowed a mouthful. Her eyes watered and she coughed.

Nick's hand shot to Joy's back. He was just as quick at it as Diana was.

"Do you want some water?" Kevin asked solicitously, while Diana and Nick patted Joy's back.

Joy shook her head and elbowed both Nick and Diana away. "It went down wrong." Joy coughed again. "That's all."

With determined aplomb, Joy lifted the hand still gripping the margarita and took a sip. A very tiny sip. Just enough to defiantly prove she was fine.

Nick caught the triumphant look Joy didn't know was in her eyes as she put the glass down on the table without coughing or getting teary this time. He wanted to hug her. He intended to do just that as soon as he could get her on the dance floor again. *Just how long a break did the band take?*

Diana's attention was still on Joy. "I hope you don't intend to finish that drink."

"Leave your sister alone," Kevin piped up. "At some point we have to let both these fledglings find their own way."

Nick grinned. "Does that mean I don't have to hear any more lectures from you about how I'm running my life? Or was that ruining my life?"

"I'll discuss that with you tomorrow after I've read the terms of the sale," Kevin countered. "It was taking chances with your life. Just to set the record straight."

"Is everything set for the wedding?" Nick asked, switching the focus.

"Well . . ." Diana pondered. "I have to take Rachel tomorrow morning to be fitted for her bridesmaid's dress. Thank heavens, Ms. Louella has another gown in the shop to match the others."

Diana turned winsome eyes to Kevin. "Don't say anything. I know I keep changing my mind, but I'm still not sure about the floral arrangements. I've decided to take you and my mother with me Saturday morning. I promise I'll make my final decision then."

Kevin grinned. "I'm not saying anything."

"I'll go with you again, if you want me to go," Joy said. "I won't even try to push my opinion on you."

"What kind of flowers do you like?" Nick asked Joy.

"Red roses with white carnations and lots of green," Joy said dreamily. "It is a Christmas wedding."

Diana sighed. "I like red and white, but what if a lot of people wear navy blue? It will look like flag day."

Kevin teasingly tweaked Diana's nose. "What's wrong with being patriotic?"

"I don't want my wedding patriotic. I want it romantic. I can't believe I have no trouble at all making decisions for my clients."

Kevin's brown eyes gazed tenderly at his wife-to-be. "I love you getting crazy over our wedding. Are we still set to take your mother to visit your uncle Terry in the afternoon?"

"Yes." Diana gazed back at Kevin. "You don't mind driving all the way up to Yonkers, do you? My uncle Terry really wants to meet you, and he's not going to be able to make it to the wedding with his leg in a cast."

Kevin smiled. "I'd drive to the ends of the earth for you."

Joy sat observing Diana and Kevin, thinking how hard this must be on Nick. She could imagine what he was going through.

"Did Eddie make any headway today?" Kevin asked, looking like he'd just suddenly realized that he and Diana weren't alone.

Nick cast Joy a sidelong glance, his mind putting a different spin on Kevin's question. Eddie's headway was blocked tonight, but that was just tonight.

She was looking down at her drink. He knew she didn't want to drink any more of it.

"He's getting there," Diana answered.

"If he started in the morning and not late afternoon, he'd be finished already," Kevin said, speaking to Nick. "You've got to see the way he works. He paints a quarter of a wall and stands back to admire it for twenty minutes. Do you remember how fast we used to paint a room for Mom?"

Nick nodded his head, savoring the pleasant memory.

"You can't rush an artist," Diana insisted. "He's doing a fantastic job. Don't you think so, Joy?"

"Fantastic," Joy answered, preoccupied. She was debating whether or not to try another sip of the margarita.

Kevin smiled at Diana. "What about the menu? Have we finished debating that?"

"The menu . . ." Diana let out a moan. "Right. We haven't finished deciding on the menu."

"What we should do is have Nick help us decide," Kevin suggested. "How about we all go to the restaurant for dinner on Sunday? Okay with you, Nick?"

"It's good for me, if it's good for Joy."

Joy's eyes went to Nick. "It's fine with me." What was one more night of the Nick, Kevin and Diana saga?

"I'll ask Rachel to come along," Diana added enthusiastically. "And Mother, of course."

Joy pushed back her seat and stood. "I'm going to finish my drink at the bar. I really should keep Eddie company for a while."

Nick's good mood took a dive. "It's still pretty hectic at the bar."

"It's eased up some." She wanted to be away from Nick. Between nearly falling over herself while they'd been dancing and then coughing over her drink, this was not one of her better nights. To sit and listen as Diana extolled Rachel, which Joy was certain Diana was going to do, was more than she could take.

Nick tried to come up with something else to say to keep Joy from going to the bar, but nothing came into his head.

"I can't wait for you to meet Rachel," Diana said, as Joy walked from the table.

"I think five heads is more than enough to vote on your wedding menu," Nick replied impatiently, turning in his seat to better keep his eye on Joy. He watched as she took a seat at the bar and began talking to a clearly pleased Eddie.

Nick took a pull on his bottle of beer. Then his view of Joy was blocked as a couple came to stand behind her.

"I still can't get over your buying the *Greenport News*," Kevin said. "I hope you haven't jumped before thinking it through. I *know* how you are."

"I'm not flying by the seat of my pants anymore," Nick replied. "I had been giving a lot of thought to staying put in one place for a while now."

"It still seems to me that you got on this rather suddenly." Kevin gave Nick his legal-eagle look.

"How did you know the paper was for sale? Did you make an inquiry?"

"Something like that." Nick restlessly tapped his index finger on the table. "How long do you think it's going to be before the group starts playing again?"

Kevin shrugged his shoulders.

Diana did the same when she noted Kevin glance at his watch. "You really have more work you want to get to tonight, don't you?"

Kevin smiled. "It's okay. I'll give myself an extra hour in the morning."

"I don't want you having to get up an hour earlier. If you leave now you'll be able to finish up whatever you have left."

"Are you sure you don't mind?"

Diana leaned toward Kevin and placed a quick kiss on his mouth. "Go home," she ordered lovingly.

Nick watched the interplay between Diana and Kevin. They were going to make it, he thought. They really had it right.

Kevin stood and put on his coat. "I'll say goodnight to Joy on my way out. Sleep well, sweetheart. Nick, I'll call you as soon as I've read through the papers."

Nick smiled. "Don't burn the midnight oil too long."

"Now who's lecturing?" Kevin replied with a farewell wave of his hand.

Diana and Nick watched Kevin leave. He pushed between the couple behind Joy to say good-night, then headed out the door.

The singer took her place again on the platform, and the group started to play. Nick cursed their timing.

He couldn't very well leave Diana to herself and ask Joy to dance. *Yeah, Tremain. And what makes you think she wants to dance with you?*

"Would you mind if we left soon?" Diana asked. "I don't want to get to bed too late."

"I'm ready any time you and Joy are." As far as Nick could see, the rest of the evening was ruined.

Diana got to her feet. "Could you see if Joy is ready? I'm just going to the ladies' room."

Nick headed for the bar while Diana headed in the opposite direction to the rest rooms.

"How about Friday night?" Eddie was asking Joy as Nick came up behind her. "And we'll go somewhere after I finish up. I understand you don't want to stay out late during the week, but you can't tell me you have to get up early Saturday morning."

"As a matter of fact, I do have to get up early Saturday morning. I promised Diana that I'd go with her to check on the flowers for the wedding."

Nick heard enough of the conversation to know Joy was shooting Eddie down. It was a sterling moment for Nick.

"Hey, Nick," Eddie said, fighting a glower as he acknowledged Nick's presence.

Joy twisted her head around, startled. She hadn't realized he was behind her. "Where's Diana?"

"She went to the ladies' room. She's ready to leave. Are you ready?" He put a hand on her arm.

Joy nodded. The hand he'd placed so nonchalantly on her arm made her heart race.

"Hey, it's not even ten o'clock," Eddie protested. "Let Diana go with Nick. I'll take you home. I'm not going to work that late. Gillie will let me go."

Joy swung off her stool. "I'm already kind of tired."

"How about Saturday night?" Eddie asked. "I'll hold a table right up front for you."

On reflection, Joy didn't want to be sitting home like a wallflower on Saturday night. Certainly not in front of Nick. By then he'd probably be dating Rachel, though he'd still be in love with Diana.

"All right." Joy proffered Eddie a very feminine smile, which threw Nick for a loop. Hadn't she just been shooting Eddie DeMarco down?

"See you at the house tomorrow night," Eddie said, as he was summoned by an annoyed customer at the bar.

"So you're coming here to hear Eddie sing Saturday night?" Nick asked stiffly.

"Yes," Joy responded blithely, walking with him toward the table. "You could get a date and come along if you like. Diana does see Kevin on the weekend, but Rachel isn't going with anyone right now."

"I might just do that," Nick replied dryly, the prospect only of interest because he didn't see any other choice if he planned on tagging after her.

"Are we leaving?" Diana asked, as she arrived back at the table.

"We're leaving," Nick answered tightly.

"I'll take Eddie over his jacket,' Joy said, after quickly picking her coat out from the pile and putting it on.

Nick held Diana's coat for her. He'd intended to do the same for Joy, but she hadn't given him a chance. Couldn't she see that Eddie DeMarco was all wrong for her?

Joy was waiting at the door, and Nick escorted both women out. The car he'd rented at the airport was parked six cars down from the door of Gillie's. It was windy and icy cold outside. Nick noticed Diana crossed her hands over her head to keep her hair in place while Joy's hair blew every which way as her hands were girded around her chest to keep warm. He thought of putting his arm around her, but didn't try. How much of a jerk was he looking to make of himself? If she wanted Eddie, she wanted Eddie.

Joy stood aside along with Diana while Nick swung open the passenger door and the back seat door. Automatically Joy got into the back. Just as automatically Diana sat down in front.

Nick closed both doors and went around to the driver's side. He started the car, put the heater on and adjusted the rearview mirror to cover more of the back seat.

Joy's eyes met his in the rearview mirror. She could see herself, as well, and just how wild the wind had made her hair. She did what she could to fix it with her fingers.

"I can't wait for Kevin to see my wedding gown," Diana said, beginning a conversation while Nick drove. And Joy just sat.

"I'm still worried about tripping over the train," Diana continued.

"You're not going to trip over the train," Joy assured her sister as Diana looked back to her for a guarantee.

"I hope not," Diana said with a sigh, facing forward again.

Joy imagined herself in Diana's wedding gown. It was exactly the gown she would have chosen for herself. She had in fact been the one to select it for Diana.

Nick turned the radio on, as Diana grew quiet.

Joy leaned her head on an angle upon the seat of the car. Tired, Joy closed her eyes.

"Nick says he's willing to carry you upstairs." Diana leaned toward Joy, shaking her elbow gently. "Do you want to get up? Or do you want Nick to demonstrate his muscles?" There was a giggle in Diana's voice.

"What!" Joy rose with a start. "Are we home?"

Diana nodded and backed out of the door, making way as Nick reached in to help Joy out of the car.

Joy pushed his hands aside, getting out on her own. She was shaky as she stood.

"It's freezing," Diana said over her shoulder, rushing up the driveway to the front door.

A gust of wind nearly knocked Joy over.

Nick caught Joy to him with one arm, bracketing her against his side. "I really wouldn't mind carrying you." His voice was soft, low and sexy.

"Find yourself some other way to show off for Diana," Joy snapped, pulling free to walk on her own. She was as much cranky as she was tired. And she was good and angry. Somehow she'd started dating Eddie DeMarco again. She didn't want to be dating Eddie DeMarco.

Once in the house she marched past Nick and Diana and went straight up the stairs not bothering to take off her coat.

Diana opened the hall closet and hung up her coat. "I'm going up. Are you?"

Nick was too edgy to even think of going to sleep. "Not yet."

"Well, good night. I'll see you tomorrow."

"Good night."

Nick took off his jacket, hung it up, then checked his watch. It was a little after eleven. Taking his wallet from the back pocket of his slacks, Nick pulled out his phone calling card. He went into the kitchen and dialed.

"Hello," Teddy Falco said, after the fourth ring.

"You can kill me if I woke you," Nick said contritely. He'd been just about to hang up.

"Nick?"

"Yeah."

"If you were here I could kill you," Teddy ribbed. "In what godforsaken place are you?"

"I'm on Long Island. In Greenport. Did I wake up Quinn?" Nick asked, referring to Teddy's wife.

"You didn't wake either one of us up."

"Don't tell me I broke the mood?"

Teddy laughed. "Don't worry. I'm not going to kill you. We're always in the mood."

Nick grinned. "I'll call you back in the morning."

"Quinn just banged me in the head with a pillow." There was a chortle in Teddy's voice. "She wants you to know we were not doing anything. I was talking rock and roll to her and she was telling me about a ballet she wants to see. What are you doing with yourself in Greenport?"

"My brother is getting married here, and I bought a newspaper. I'll tell you all about it some other time.

Right now I need a favor from you. It's a big one. Feel free to say no."

"Go ahead. I'll say no if I feel the need."

"There's a rock singer. His name is Eddie De-Marco. He's opening up at a place called Gillie's in Westhampton tomorrow night. I'd like him booked on a West Coast tour. Can you arrange it?"

"Is he good?" Teddy asked.

"I have no idea," Nick admitted.

"Let me guess," Teddy bantered. "There's a woman involved and this guy is muscling in."

Nick groaned. "Exactly."

"They never have any idea how much we guys suffer over them."

"Am I stepping on your toes?" Nick asked.

"Yeah," Teddy laughed. "But I do remember a few times I stepped on yours. What are friends for?"

"Can you do it?"

"Sure. I know plenty of joints on the West Coast. How soon do you want him gone?"

"Yesterday," Nick answered comically.

"I'll catch his act tomorrow night."

"I don't want him knowing it came from me."

"Gotcha."

"Thanks, Teddy," Nick said, as Diana walked into the kitchen.

"Night, pal." Teddy rang off.

Nick hung up on his end.

"Was that your friend Teddy?" Diana asked, taking a container from the refrigerator.

"Uh-huh," Nick said uncomfortably.

Diana poured herself a half a glass of juice. "Do you want some?"

Nick shook his head.

"I remember we went out with your friend Teddy and his wife once. They're very nice."

"Yes, they are." Nick raked his fingers through his thick hair. What were the chances of her remembering that Teddy was a music-business agent and promoter?

Diana downed her juice. "Now I think I can sleep. Good night again."

"Good night."

Nick stood there debating whether or not to call Teddy back and cancel out.

Chapter Five

"Between yesterday and today, I've got some really great material," Joy said animatedly, looking over at Nick from the passenger seat of the sports car he'd leased the day before to replace the car he'd rented at the airport.

Nick smiled. "I didn't think it was going to do much for the story to include a winery that hasn't marketed a single bottle yet, but I take it back. It was a stroke of genius on your part. You're really good at this." He'd had his first opportunity to watch her do an interview. And she'd bowled him over.

"Thanks. I love when it happens this way, when you get material you haven't expected."

He could see that she'd liked his compliment. "Those in-depth questions of yours got right to the heart and soul. The owner here has a really colorful past. It didn't look like he was going to be forthcoming at all, but you worked away at him without him even knowing he was being handled, and you got him to open up."

He hadn't yet turned the key in the ignition. They were finished for the day. The winery was closing, and it had just started to snow—lightly—the first snow of the season.

"I know the pictures you took for me today are going to make the story much more than it is," Joy said. It was even tougher than she'd expected, to keep herself in a business frame of mind around him. "I think it's important that people understand all that a winery owner has riding on his business. A sizable investment can be wiped out by the whim of a bad winter or too much rain."

"Or too much sun," Nick said lazily. *Way to go, Tremain. You, rascal, you.*

"Or too much sun," Joy concurred. She knew he wasn't referring to the trials and tribulations of making a winery pay off. He was referring to the beach in East Hampton. *What did he want from her?*

Joy hugged her arms together. "Well..." Her hands got lost in the sleeves of her coat like a muffler, as she clasped them together in front of her waist.

"Are you cold?"

"Not really," Joy answered, staring straight ahead. The snow was beginning to cover the front window. The muscles in her lower abdomen were shivery, but not because she was cold. "I sampled enough wine in the last two days to keep myself warm for a while."

"And Diana said you couldn't handle your wine," he teased, with one arm draped over the wheel, his back to the driver's door.

"To be perfectly honest, I am a little tipsy." Joy wondered if he had any sense of her tension. Sitting alone with him in his car with the sky darkening around them was very intimate.

"How tipsy?" Nick asked, clearly amused, though his eyes had taken on a sultry look.

"You don't have to worry until my eyes cross," Joy answered, getting impudent with him. It was as good a way as she could think of to cover her nervousness.

"You're too far away for me to check that out for myself." His fingers circled her neck, while his other hand slid around her waist where her hands were girded together. He towed her slowly toward him until the gearshift between their seats held him back.

"Are they crossed?" Joy asked breathlessly. She knew it wasn't her eyes he was interested in playfully exploring. Oh, she was such a weakling.

Nick slowly shook his head, and then he smiled that damnable sexy smile of his.

The instant his mouth settled onto hers, Joy's eyes closed and her lips parted for him. She felt his tongue reach toward her own, felt hers respond.

He released her neck, taking her into her arms to pull her closer against his leather jacket. She gave him permission as her hands unwound from the fortress she'd made in front of her waist.

Joy wrapped her hands low around his hips. Her tongue was moving along with his in sensual circles within her mouth. He put a few inches between their bodies to bring one hand to the front of her coat. She sensed that he'd finished opening the buttons even before his hand came over one breast to cup her gently against the fabric of her blouse and bra. Her imagination—and it had run creatively rampant—had in no way prepared her for what it would actually feel like to have him touch her this way. Joy thought she'd actually stopped breathing. She was completely unaware she was moaning. Or that his other hand had slid inside her coat and was tugging her blouse out of her skirt. Lost in passion and emotion, Joy initiated her own racing need to touch. Tentatively Joy brought a hand up inside his unzipped jacket to his chest, moving his tie aside to slip a trembling finger between the buttons of his blue shirt.

At the realization of what she was attempting to do, he stopped kissing her and leaned back just enough to give her more access.

"Go ahead," Nick whispered raggedly, his breath whisking across her face as he finished tugging her blouse out of her skirt.

Joy didn't feel what he was doing with her blouse. The only thing she felt was his shudder as she opened a button of his shirt. Remembering the way he'd looked without a shirt, his chest entirely exposed, Joy opened another button. It was too dark in the car for her to see all she wanted to see, but touching was no problem at all. She pressed her palm to hard muscle. Her fingers fanned out. She found a nipple and timorously touched the tip.

His breath was painfully constricting but neither hell nor high water could have kept Nick from lifting up her blouse now. He bunched the hem in his hand and brought it up.

A guttural groan came from his throat. He sought the clasp of her bra and released it. "I love you, Joy."

His words broke through the fog that was Joy's mind.

"Really?" Joy asked sarcastically, knowing the truth. He was trying to do exactly what Eddie had suggested. He wanted to use her to make Diana jealous.

"Yes," Nick said simply, stock-still now, trying to understand the inflection of her voice.

Joy yanked her blouse out of his hand. She couldn't even blame him for what had been going on. It was her own fault that she'd allowed him to take advantage of her vulnerability.

"What's wrong?" Nick asked, bewildered. Wasn't the declaration he'd given her the declaration every woman wanted to hear? Was she thinking he just bandied the words around?

Giving no response at all, except to glare at him, Joy finished backing herself up against the passenger door.

"Don't you believe me?" He was able to make out that she was trying futilely to hook her bra. "I really do love you."

Joy grimaced. She'd have to be even more stupid than she already was to fall for that. God! He even had the right tone of voice!

She was all disheveled. Her coat was in her way. She couldn't hook her bra. " 'You can fool some of the people...' "

At that, Nick cut her off. "Could we leave famous quotes out of this? What do you want me to do? Write it in blood?"

"That's a thought," Joy said furiously, then used an expletive under her breath when she still couldn't get her bra clasped. Joy angrily pulled her coat up from under her and tried again to fasten her bra.

Nick pulled in a breath that covered the range from impatience to frustration. "Turn around and I'll do it for you." He had a knee rammed hard against the gearshift. *You can fool some of the people,* Nick repeated antagonistically in his head.

"I can do it myself," Joy retorted.

"Fine." Nick sucked in another frustrated breath.

Joy finally got the clasp hooked and began vehemently pushing her pink silk blouse into the band of her black wool skirt. "Should I find someplace to call for a taxi? Or are you planning to drive?"

Her voice snapped at him like a rubber band.

Biting down on his lip, Nick started the car and slid the heater level to its highest setting. He was almost tempted to take her up on her dare. She had him that nuts!

Nick opened his door and slammed out of the car. Joy saw his face again a second later as the arm of his leather jacket swept through the snow across the front window. The winery was lit up outdoors.

For the fraction of a moment, blatantly irritated blue eyes met conspicuously angry gray-green eyes.

Joy opened her door and got one foot out. Her high heel sank into the snow.

"What do you think you're doing?" Nick blocked her way in a flash.

"I'm going to help clear the windows," Joy answered acerbically.

"No, you're not!"

"Yes, I am!" Joy got her other foot out of the car nearly kicking Nick in the shin as she did so.

"And you've called me obstinate!" He put his hands to her hips to get her seated again.

"Believe me, you are!" Joy fired back. "Will you let go of me?"

"If you don't sit back down, I'm going to pick you up and sit you down!"

You and who else? was the retort that came into her head, but Joy had just enough sense left to keep from saying it out loud.

"I'm going to give you to the count of three. One..." Nick began.

Joy sat back down just as he reached three. She stamped her high heels to the carpet under her feet and bent forward to rub circulation back into her ankles and insteps.

"Turn the wipers on," Nick requested tersely, when she straightened up.

Joy reached out and flippantly turned the wipers on. Nick closed her door, not all that gently.

When Nick got in behind the wheel, his hands were almost frostbitten. He steepled his fingers together in front of his face and blew into his palms, then he held his hands to the blower of the heater.

"I could drive," Joy volunteered, barely louder than a whisper, feeling very upset at how much his hands must be stinging. It required all her teeth-gritting strength not to reach for his hands and rub them between hers.

Nick tossed Joy a vexed look. "No, thanks."

"Okay." She used the same nasty voice he'd used on her.

Nick put a hand to the wheel and the other to the gearshift. He backed out of the parking slot with the tires spinning, his fingers still cold, but his disposition steaming.

The half hour trip to the house passed in tight, strained silence.

Nick braked on the driveway and turned the motor off. His car was behind Joy's car, which was in back of Diana's car. It was still snowing, and what had already come down had covered the asphalt and the lawn.

"Tell me where your boots are. I'll go in and get them for you."

Joy mulled over his thoughtful suggestion for a second. Only she was too angry to give him as much as an inch. Besides, his offer hadn't been delivered all that politely.

With her head tilted at its most stubborn angle, Joy countered, "I can make it without boots."

Joy had her car door opened and was gingerly stepping out and into the snow when Nick reached her.

"You're going to fall if you try to walk on your own in those shoes." He adamantly fixed his arm around her waist, forcing her to lean into him.

"I don't need your help!" Joy tried spiritedly to free herself.

"If you don't quit fighting me, I'm going to lift you up and carry you into the house." Nick held onto Joy even tighter.

"Pul-eeze... Not the Tarzan bit!" Joy rammed her elbow into his flat abs, trying to get at him through his jacket. It was that expenditure of temper that sent her feet sliding. She went down on her rear end, which was luckily padded by her coat. Nick went down with her.

"Are you hurt anywhere?" Nick questioned anxiously.

"No," Joy replied limply. She doubted he was inquiring about her heart. "Are you hurt?"

"No," Nick responded, rising up on one knee. "Move your legs a little. Just a little. Let me know if you feel any pain."

Joy moved her legs like a pair of scissors, looking them over as she did. "Oh . . ." she moaned.

"What?" Nick gasped.

"My nylons are all shredded."

Nick released the breath that had gotten hung up in his throat. She was impossible! She was obstinate to the umpteenth degree. Frustrating beyond belief. And he was wild about her.

Nick squatted on the balls of his feet. "Are you going to stop giving me a hard time and let me help you into the house?"

Joy weakly nodded her head. The fall had knocked the verve out of her.

Without giving her a chance to change her mind, Nick spread his hands and stood, then scooped Joy up in his arms.

"I didn't mean this way," Joy said, though she didn't move to fight him this time.

The lights over the garage and the front door threw quite a bit of light on the driveway. She could see Nick grin and she tried to shoot him a killing look. But she was expending all her effort trying to ignore the flush going through her entire body and the riotous feelings that went along with the compromising position he had her in. It wasn't fair that he was so sexy. Or that his gallantry overwhelmed her. It was punishingly unfair of him to say he loved her!

"Put your arms around my neck," Nick demanded, his smile still in place. He looked into her adorably gorgeous face and waited, without moving, for her to obey.

Joy's arms went around his neck, but she gave him another shoot-to-kill glare.

"I think the Tarzan bit does work on you." Nick quirked a grin, sparring expertly against the look he was getting from her.

"I am not at all impressed," Joy mumbled, avoiding his eyes by turning her face into his jacket. It was easier for her to lie when she wasn't looking at him.

Treading slowly, Nick carefully carried Joy across the driveway and up the stairs of the front porch, putting her down on her feet at the door.

"Don't I get a thank you?"

"Thank you," Joy said through her teeth. She went to turn the knob of the door, but Nick put his hand to hers, stopping her.

"I'm not taking back what I said to you before," Nick murmured gruffly, gazing into her vibrant gray-green eyes.

Joy flipped her head aside. "You can say it all you want. It's not going to work for you."

"What's not going to work?" His breath mingled with hers in the air.

"I am not going to let you use me to try and make Diana jealous." Joy spelled it out for him, though she didn't think it was necessary for her to do so. It did salve her pride some that she could tell him she knew what he was up to.

"You've got it all wrong." He brought his face down to her face and said it close to her mouth.

For a second Joy thought he was going to kiss her again. Her heart jumped excitedly into her throat. But he didn't.

Nick lifted his head and held her eyes with his. "I'm going to tell you one more time. The only interest I have in Diana is as my future sister-in-law. I'm in love with you. And I know you're at least attracted to me."

"Where's a lie detector when you need one?" Joy asked sassily, trying to save herself. Speculating on the possibility that he really meant that he loved her was ludicrous. She'd lost her heart, but she hadn't lost her mind. "And don't be so sure I'm attracted to you. I'm not! It was the wine. I must have had one taste too many."

"Like hell." Nick bent his head again and this time he did kiss her. Thoroughly. And, weakling that she was, Joy responded right back.

"Do you want to tell me again that you're not attracted to me?" Nick asked, pulling slightly away from her.

"It's still the wine." Joy fiercely turned the knob of the door and pushed it open. She knew he had a smile on his face as he stepped inside after her.

"You!" Diana came whirling into the front hallway with her finger pointed at Nick.

"What's the matter?" Joy asked, her eyes wide.

Emily Mackey was coming down the stairs, carrying towels. "Diana, let's all go into the kitchen. Joy and Nick, you can take your coat and jacket off in there and dry your hair. Then you can all talk."

With the towels in her hands, Emily Mackey started the parade off for the kitchen. Diana threw Nick another riveting look before following her mother.

"What did you do to Diana?" Joy asked Nick in an anxious whisper as the two lagged behind.

"Beats me," Nick whispered back, lost out in left field for the second time this evening. Had someone hung a sign on his back and declared open season?

Joy was working at the buttons of her coat with frozen fingers but sweating palms, as she took off after Diana and her mother.

Nick brought up the rear, trying to guess what might have gotten Diana all turned out. He hadn't seen her since the evening before. There hadn't been any problem then.

Emily gave Nick and her daughter towels after they'd hung their outerwear up on pegs next to the back door.

"All right, Diana. What is it?" Nick asked, after roughing his hair up with the towel, then stringing the towel around his neck.

Joy still had her towel plopped over her head, needing longer to tend to the mass of her hair.

"Eddie DeMarco called this morning," Diana began in a very tight voice, like she was trying to keep herself from going ballistic. "He didn't come to paint today. In fact, he's not going to be able to finish painting. He quit Gillie's, too, because he had to leave with his group for California immediately."

Nick was watching Diana and listening. So far it was no major news. He'd been certain Teddy would come through. "Is this about Eddie not being able to finish the painting?"

"Why should that be a big concern?" Diana rejoined, near to hysterics. "I'm only supposed to get
married here in less than three weeks."

"There are plenty of painters around." He felt like
he was back in the middle of a war zone ducking bul-
lets while all he had to aim with was his camera.

Diana's blue eyes snapped. "I've been on the phone
all day. There isn't anyone available right this minute.
Did you check that out, too, before you spoke to your
friend Teddy?"

Joy finished drying her hair. "I don't understand
what Nick has to do with this. Who is Teddy?"

"Teddy Falco is a friend of Nick's," Diana responded. "He handles rock singers. Teddy Falco is the
one who is giving Eddie and his group this big break
after he came to see them open last night. Eddie just
happened to mention the name of his new agent."

"That could just be a coincidence," Joy defended.
"What makes you think Nick had something to do
with it?"

"I'll tell you how I know," Diana said. "I just
happened to walk into the kitchen Monday night after we got home from Gillie's, and Nick was getting
off the phone with Teddy Falco."

"I'll finish the painting," Nick said, beyond just
plain exasperation. "I'll do it Saturday. I can finish it
all up in one day. You can take my word for it."

"I'll help," Joy said, intending to make certain the
painting did get done. Diana had been absolutely right
to have been worried. Nick *had* looked for a way to try
and mess up the wedding and found one.

Nick's first thought was that Joy was offering her
assistance because she wanted to be with him. The

smile he turned to give her froze before it got to his mouth. From the militant expression on her face, it was abundantly clear that wanting to be with him wasn't her goal.

Emily Mackey stepped in to give her motherly input to her oldest daughter. "I'm sure Nick was only trying to do Eddie a good turn, just as Kevin said. There was no need for you to get upset. It's very nice of Nick to be willing to help out with the painting. I'm certain he'll do an excellent job. Eddie was taking entirely too long, anyway. Call Kevin back and tell him that everything is fine. Joy and Nick, go upstairs and change. Dinner is ready. My goodness, Joy. I hope you didn't walk around with your stockings in that condition all day."

"No, Mom. It just happened." Joy gave her head a little shake, hoping to clear it of everything else that had happened to her sitting in the car with You-Can-Take-My-Word-for-It Nick Tremain.

"I can explain," Nick insisted to Joy, after they'd left the kitchen.

Joy spun around to him. "Are you going to tell me you were just trying to do Eddie a favor?"

"No," Nick answered truthfully.

"Good. I wouldn't want you to waste your breath." Joy pivoted back around and marched upstairs.

Now, Nick concluded, was not the right time to try to reason with her.

Chapter Six

"I appreciate that you haven't brought it up, Kev, but I feel I should tell you why I sent Teddy to see Eddie DeMarco." Nick kept a firm grip on Maxie's leash. "I wasn't trying to do Eddie a favor."

"I know," Kevin responded, as the brothers walked along in the woods behind the bed and breakfast early Saturday morning, two days after the incident. "You sent Teddy Falco to get Eddie out of your way."

Nick stopped short, cutting off Maxie's rollicking progress. The dog yanked at the leash.

Kevin turned to Nick. "You want a clear path to Joy."

Nick's startled eyes met his brother's smiling ones. "Exactly," Nick conceded with a grin.

"I knew I was right," Kevin said smugly.

"If you figured it out, how come you didn't explain it to Diana?"

"Telling Diana is the same as telling Joy. I thought you'd want to take care of that yourself. *Have* you told Joy how you feel?"

"Oh, yeah." Nick let a breath out through his teeth. "I told her that I'm in love with her. She doesn't believe me. She's got it in her head that I'm still interested in Diana. She thinks I want to use her to make Diana jealous."

Kevin fixed his lawyer stare on Nick. "You are positive that you're over Diana?"

"I've already told you that, Kev," Nick replied, clearly vexed.

Kevin put his hands up in a gesture of surrender. "Just giving it one more check."

"I'm glad you haven't said anything to Diana. I'm clearly not in your fiancée's graces."

"Don't take Diana's attitude toward you to heart. She hasn't got her head on straight right now. Women and weddings." Kevin sighed happily. "Half the time I'm feeling left out of it."

Nick grinned. "You've got your work cut out for you remembering where to stand and when to say 'I do.' That's enough for any guy to handle."

Kevin kiddingly socked Nick's upper arm. "You could do me a favor."

"Name it," Nick smiled.

"Let Diana help you find a house to rent. She needs to get her focus off this wedding a little and it will give the two of you something to bond over. Nick, I want you and Diana to really be friends."

"All right, I'll ask Diana for her input," Nick agreed. "How about a favor for a favor?"

"Name it," Kevin smiled.

"Don't come back too early from Yonkers tonight. In fact, how about stopping for a long, leisurely dinner, then maybe a late movie? That will give me plenty of time alone with Joy."

"I planned on dinner." Kevin grinned. "I'll see what I can do about a movie. Shall we go back inside? They should be downstairs by now."

Diana and her mother were putting their coats on in the front hallway as Nick and Kevin came through the door. Joy was standing with them, wearing an inside-out sweatshirt over abused jeans. She was dressed to paint.

Nick's eyes veered right to Joy.

Joy's eyes veered instantly away from Nick's.

Maxie bounded up the stairs to the TV room where his bowl of water and food were set out.

"My mother wanted to make breakfast," Diana said to Kevin. "I'd rather get started. Do you mind if we have something out?"

"I don't mind at all." Kevin smiled at both Diana and his future mother-in-law.

"Joy, I almost forgot," Diana said in a rush. "I called House of Brides. Ms. Louella wasn't in yet. I left word for her to call here about my gown. I know I've been talking about it and talking about it, but I'm sure now. I want it up three inches. I had the worst nightmare last night about tripping over myself. Will you tell her to shorten it?"

"Three inches. I'll tell her," Joy confirmed, as Kevin herded Diana and her mother out the door.

Surreptitiously, Joy watched Nick take off his leather jacket and hang it up in the closet. He had on just a white T-shirt and jeans. His jeans were equally faded and worn, but molded more to his hips, thighs and legs than hers were. He had his back to her, and Joy could see another part of him where his jeans fit well.

Joy pulled nonchalantly on the already-out-of-shape neckline of her sweatshirt. She was thinking about how unsexy she looked.

The neckline dipped lower on one shoulder, exposing the strap of her red bra. Joy helped the revelation along even more by seesawing her posture just as he turned from the closet.

His eyes got held up just where she'd hoped they would.

"Do your panties match?" Nick asked, wearing a rowdy smile. The little minx! He hadn't been able to see the strap of her bra a minute ago. She was showing it to him.

Joy gave an Oscar-winning performance of naïveté, following his gaze to her shoulder, and acting abashed at finding out what he was seeing. "Whether my panties match or not is something you'll never know," Joy answered pluckily, adjusting her neckline.

"You know what happens when a bull sees red?" His blue eyes got bluer. "He charges." Nick teasingly pitched forward.

Joy backed up a big step, though she didn't really want to. "Are we going to paint?" she asked. "You did give your word that you were going to get the painting done today. You do mean everything you say, don't you?"

Nick grinned and straightened. "I don't think I'll bite on that bait. But I will say I prefer you being riled at me, than getting the cold shoulder you've been giving for the past two days."

"I have not been giving you a cold shoulder," Joy insisted. "I was busy working on my story. How would you know, anyway? You've been in your office most of the past two days." And after dinner he'd taken to his room to continue editing other reporters' contributions.

"Have you missed me?" He was no longer teasing; he was begging.

"No," Joy lied aloofly. "Are we ready to paint?"

"I've missed you," Nick whispered.

"Really?" Joy's eyes met his, moved away, then met his again. She fidgeted with her hair. She fidgeted with her sweatshirt. This being alone with him was not her most brilliant idea.

"Really."

Joy dropped her gaze. She'd pulled on her sweatshirt so much it was almost down over her knees. You have got to be a sight to behold, Joy thought self-critically, while she tried to right her shirt. Her breathing was irregular. Did he really expect her to believe him?

"I haven't had coffee yet. Have you?" Nick pushed his fingers through his wind-ruffled hair.

"No." Joy brought her eyes up to his, a good amount of her natural tenacity back in place.

"I'll put on a pot." Nick took her expression as a cue that he wasn't going to get any further with her right now.

"It was very nice of you to bring in all those groceries last night," Joy said, speaking at random as they walked to the kitchen. She'd meant to tell him so last night, but she hadn't been able to get a word in above her mother's protestations that it hadn't been necessary for him to stuff the refrigerator and freezer.

Nick stopped for a moment, looked at her and smiled. "Is that really *you* calling *me* nice?"

"I'm just confirming how my mother feels about you," Joy answered flippantly as they entered the kitchen. "She thinks you're absolutely charming. She thought so even before you brought in the groceries. In fact, she thought so all the way back to the first time she met you."

"I hope you've inherited some of your mother's good taste." Nick sent a grin over his shoulder on his way to the cabinet for the coffee.

"I'm not very easily charmed," Joy countered, liking her retort.

"Tell me about it." Nick exaggerated a groan as he flipped open the can of coffee at the counter.

Joy went to the refrigerator and took out a box of doughnuts that he'd brought in last night. "Doughnuts, okay?" she asked.

"Sure," Nick answered.

Joy moved around the kitchen, feeling too antsy to sit. She was waiting for him to say something smart-alecky to her that she could respond to.

"We probably should have something more substantial than doughnuts," Joy said, breaking through the quiet while Nick poured the coffee that had just finished dripping. "I could scramble up some eggs." He hadn't said anything to her at all.

"Okay." Nick turned with two cups of black coffee in his hands. He knew she took her coffee without milk and sugar, just like he did. "Have your coffee and doughnut first, and I'll do the eggs with you."

Joy made a face. "It doesn't take two people to scramble eggs."

"I'll crack. You can scramble. Sit." He motioned with his head to the table and chairs.

"Has anyone told you that you're very bossy?" Joy parried, taking a seat.

Nick slid Joy a devilish look. "I bought the title." He took the chair next to hers and put both cups down.

"It doesn't cover you on the weekend." Joy volleyed this back as she picked up her coffee.

Nick opened the box of assorted doughnuts. "I've got a few other tactics up my sleeve to get you to do my bidding." He held the box of doughnuts out to her.

"Such as?" Joy challenged capriciously while she selected a cinnamon doughnut.

He took his sweet time about answering, and when he did, he didn't answer her question at all. "Do you know that that doughnut is the color of your hair?"

Joy's eyelids fluttered down momentarily as she glanced at the doughnut, which was now minus a bite. "My hair is just an ordinary brown."

"There is nothing ordinary about your hair," Nick objected, capturing a wavy handful and letting it slip through his fingers. "There's nothing ordinary about the rest of you, either. Certainly not your eyes, your nose, your mouth. Definitely not that drop-dead body."

Joy's "drop-dead" body went all shivery, though she sat as still as a bird hoping to be camouflaged from a great, big tomcat.

"Wait a minute!" Joy flipped her hair with her own hand. "Is this one of your tactics?"

"No." He gave her a maverick grin. "That's on your side of the board. Did I mention you could get me to do your bidding anytime you want? All you have to do is ask." His eyes moved over her hair, cheeks, mouth—which he most certainly didn't find ordinary—before returning to her gorgeous eyes.

A stab of warmth flooded Joy's cheeks. She held a breath before letting it gush out. "I thought the line was 'All you have to do is whistle.'"

Was there a woman alive that could withstand his tactics?

Nick winked incorrigibly. "Looks like we have Bogie and Bacall in common, too. Do you know how to whistle?"

"No." Joy pushed a strand of hair away from one eye. The cup of coffee in her other hand tilted precariously. She did know how to whistle.

Nick took the coffee out of her hand and set it down. "All you have to do is put two fingers in your mouth ... and blow."

He demonstrated for her with the sexiest whistle she'd ever heard.

"Thanks for the lesson."

"You're welcome." Nick smiled. "You've got cinnamon on your lips."

Her eyes glued to his, Joy felt around for a napkin from the holder in the center of the table. Before she got to it, Nick ran his thumb seductively across her lips.

Joy's mouth dropped open, and her eyes got huge, as she watched him slowly lick his thumb. Oh God, oh God, oh God!

Nick ran his lips together. "That tasted good. Think I'll have the same." He idly took out a second cinnamon doughnut from the box.

"Stop it," Joy demanded, breathing in quick little spurts.

"You want this other cinnamon doughnut, too?" Nick asked glibly, holding it out to her. "See...all you have to do is ask."

Joy slapped the doughnut out of his hand. It flew to the floor.

Agitation and sexual tension hitting her in rapid-fire succession, Joy threw the doughnut she'd started at him. It sailed over his shoulder, missing his face, which was what she'd aimed for.

"You are a bastard!" Joy's chest was heaving.

Nick's face showed no emotion at her attack as he got up from the table and squatted next to her chair. "Why am I a bastard? Because I'm in love with you? Is that what makes me a bastard? What do I have to do to make you understand that there's no triangle here? Give me a chance, Joy. Trust me, baby. Please."

Joy couldn't look Nick in the eye. She wanted to trust what he was saying. Only she wasn't the only one who thought he was lying. Diana thought so, too.

The doorbell rang and Joy nearly jumped out of her skin.

"I'll get it," Nick said, reluctantly standing up.

Joy dropped her face to her hands after Nick left the kitchen. She took very long, very deep breaths.

"Hi," Rachel Harmon said liltingly, coming into the kitchen with Nick.

Eyes blinking, Joy quickly got to her feet. "What are you doing here?" Realizing in the next breath that she might just have sounded rude, Joy said, "What I mean is . . . I didn't expect you to come by today."

Rachel raised her hand to show Joy the paintbrush she was holding. "I was on the phone with Diana yesterday, and she told me that you and ah . . . Nick were going to be painting today. I've done some painting myself. I told Diana I'd come by and help out. Didn't she tell you?"

"No." Joy shook her head and sneaked a glance at Nick as he stood loosely on the side with his hands in the pockets of his jeans, looking at her best friend— the blond and beautiful Rachel Harmon.

"It is all right that I came by, isn't it?" Rachel asked, sharing the question between Joy and Nick.

"Of course." Joy was the one to answer, letting her dismay out on one of her long breaths. Rachel was as perfect for Nick as Diana was.

Rachel's chocolate brown eyes moved specifically to Nick.

"The more the merrier," Nick said, tossing in a smile, since agreeing appeared to be his only option. She was, he reminded himself, Joy's best friend.

"What happened here?" Rachel asked, noticing the chunks of two doughnuts on the otherwise sparkling clean floor at the same time that Joy was noting Rachel's soft, red flannel shirt tucked into blue jeans that were cinched at Rachel's very slender waist with a Western belt.

It was Nick who answered this time. "I'm a bear before I have my first cup of coffee."

Joy's nostrils flared some on her next breath. *Didn't he mean a bull?*

"I'm not sure I know what you mean," Rachel said with a smile that could have been interpreted as flirtatious.

Flirtatious was the interpretation Joy placed on it, though she did roundly reprimand herself for the sarcasm in that thought. Rachel had every right to flirt with him. Diana would be happy about it.

But Joy was miserable.

"Would you like a cup of coffee?" Joy asked Rachel in a clipped tone.

"Sure," Rachel answered, smiling with her eyes.

Joy started for the coffee maker and Nick appeared at her side.

"Point me to a broom and dustpan and I'll clean up the floor," he said, giving Joy a teasingly personal smile.

Joy squared her shoulders. She was not at all amused. "There's a broom and dustpan in the pantry." Joy pointed with her finger, her voice as stiff as her back.

"I'll hold the dustpan for you," Rachel offered quickly.

Joy poured a cup of coffee for Rachel and added a splash of milk and brought it to the table just as Nick and Rachel finished cleaning up.

The three of them sat in silence at the table. Joy glanced between Rachel and Nick as all three sipped their coffee.

Nick managed to capture Joy's eyes for just a second before she looked away. "How about I scramble up some eggs for all of us," Nick volunteered, wanting to satisfy the yen Joy had expressed earlier.

"A doughnut is enough for me," Rachel replied, helping herself to a buttermilk doughnut in the box.

Her tone cranky, Joy said, "We've wasted enough time already this morning. Let's get to the painting."

"That's the last of the paint," Nick said, swishing through the bottom of the final gallon with a brush to get the last drops into the roller pan he was using. It was late afternoon. And though they'd only taken one break for lunch there were two more walls to paint.

"We don't have anything left, either," Rachel said, looking down at the pan she and Joy were working out of to get all the molding done.

Nick unfastened the roller pad from the extension holder he'd been using and dropped it along with his paintbrush into a pail half-filled with water. "I'll go out and get another gallon."

Fast as a bunny, Rachel dropped her brush into the pail. "I'll go with you."

Joy thought about Rachel and Nick taking off together and not coming back for a good while. "Neither one of you knows which paint store Eddie was using. I'll go."

"All right," Rachel answered. "Nick and I can dry the brushes."

Joy thought about Rachel and Nick being alone in the house. That thought didn't sit any better than the thought of letting them go off together. "Rachel, you'd better come with me. I think we need more than one gallon to finish up. I'll need help carrying it.''

"One more gallon should do it," Nick said off-handedly.

Joy dug in her heels. "We can always take it back if we don't use it."

Nick read volumes, then, in Joy's eyes. As sure as he knew his own name, Nick knew she didn't want him to be alone with Rachel.

Oh, baby... Nick whistled in his head.

"You're right." He eyed a small spot of ecru paint on her chin, but he didn't do or say anything to draw her attention to it. He didn't want to douse the fire in her eyes. "We can always take back a gallon."

"Let's go," Joy said to Rachel, not about to brook any further argument even from her closest, lifelong friend—whom she did adore under other circumstances.

"Take my car," Nick said, pulling his keys from the pocket of his jeans. "I'm parked behind you."

Joy accepted the keys. She spotted a hint of teasing in his eyes that she couldn't decide how to decipher.

Nick was grinning as Joy left the house with Rachel in tow, both bundled into their coats.

He heard her gun the motor just as the phone rang.

"Hello," Nick said, picking it up.

"Diana Mackey, please. This is Ms. Louella from House of Brides. I'm returning her call."

"She's not here at the moment, but I do know what she called about." He remembered the instruction Diana had given Joy. "I'm Nick Tremain, the groom's brother. Diana wants her gown shortened three inches."

"That's impossible," Ms. Louella uttered. "What could she be thinking? It won't look right at all."

"What she's thinking about is tripping," Nick said evenly.

"You're absolutely certain she wants her gown three inches shorter?"

"I'm absolutely certain," Nick reiterated. There wasn't anything wrong with his hearing. Diana had said three inches to Joy. There wasn't any doubt in his mind about that.

"Your name again?" Ms. Louella asked in a steely tone.

"Nick Tremain."

"That's *T-r-e-m-a-i-n?*"

"Right," Nick responded.

"I'm writing your name on the slip should there be any issue later on."

"It's okay with me," Nick said, rolling his eyes at the threat.

"That does it," Nick said two hours later. He stood back, the roller in his hand, and admired the completed paint job.

"It looks great. Really great," Rachel said, gazing up at Nick from where she sat next to Joy on a drop-cloth-covered couch.

Nick's eyes were on Joy. She'd gone longer than Rachel had before she'd petered out. Nick thought about giving Joy a massage. The picture he had in his head didn't include an audience. "The question is will Diana think so?"

"She will," Joy said with a sigh, reminding herself that everything he did was for Diana.

"I think we deserve to go out and treat ourselves to a really great dinner," Rachel said, smiling at Nick before looking to Joy. "If you're too tired to go tonight, I can go with Nick, and we can all go out together another time."

Joy felt her nerves pricking over every square inch of her body. "I'm not too tired."

Nick didn't want to be impolite, but he'd gone through a whole day thinking of nothing but being alone with Joy.

"We're going to have to make it another time, Rachel. Friends of mine have already invited the two of us to dinner tonight. Isn't that right, Joy?" *Go along with me, baby. Please!*

Joy bit her lip, trying to understand this new development he'd tossed into the melee. Was he selecting her over Rachel?

So what if he was? What did that mean?

"I don't know how I could have forgotten," Joy said, when she got around to answering.

"Well..." Rachel stood. "Call me and we'll set up a date."

"Absolutely," Nick replied jubilantly.

Joy walked Rachel to the hall closet, and handed her friend her coat.

"Thanks for helping," Joy said sincerely, opening the front door.

"I didn't mind at all." Rachel glanced over Joy's shoulder to take one more look at Nick before heading out.

Joy confronted Nick as soon as she returned to the parlor. "Why did you lie to Rachel?"

Nick stretched his arms and shoulder muscles. "Why did you back me up?"

"I didn't want to hurt Rachel's feelings," Joy retorted.

"I didn't want to hurt Rachel's feelings, either," Nick countered.

Joy's eyes narrowed. "That still doesn't answer my question."

"You know the answer." He moved toward her with a prowling gait.

"Hold it right there." Joy put her hand out like a street guard halting traffic.

The gesture didn't slow Nick at all. He took the hand sticking out at him and set it around his neck. Then he wrapped his arms around her.

"Don't, Nick," Joy whispered imploringly.

He leaned to kiss her eyelids closed. First the right one, then the left.

"Don't," Joy said breathily, her eyes staying closed.

He walked her backward, manipulating her with slow, deliberate pushes of his hips and thighs against hers. He kissed the tip of her nose, peering past her cheek to the couch across the room and the stereo system that was covered up next to it.

"I mean it, Nick," Joy mumbled, while her body tingled and strained against him with each step back.

He dipped her when they got to the stereo. Raising the drop cloth with one hand, he punched the Power button, then let his eyes drift closed, kissing her mouth, all the while turning the dial until he found something soft and sexy.

"We...have...to...talk," Joy pleaded against his mouth as he brought her down on the couch with him.

She was on his lap, facing him, with her knees pressed into the cushion at either side of his hips.

Nick dropped his head back. "All right. Talk to me." His voice was thick and husky.

Joy cleared her throat. "I hate you." Both her arms were around his neck without insistence from him.

Nick smiled with his eyes closed. "No, you don't." He hauled her head down with one hand.

"I do," Joy insisted, all whispery, catching her breath as he kissed that very sensitive and vulnerable spot at the base of her throat.

"Keep talking," he teased as he lifted up her sweatshirt.

"Oh, Nick..." Joy cried out in a half sob as his mouth found the small bow at the center of her lacy red bra. Her breath rushed entirely out of her body as his tongue sought out one nipple through the lace and etched a wet mark on the spot.

"I hate your friend Rachel," Nick groaned, wishing he knew for sure how long it was going to be before Kevin came back.

"I can't believe you just said that." Joy pulled back and fiercely yanked her sweatshirt down.

"I didn't mean that literally," Nick said, silently cursing his choice of words as Joy sprang off his lap and onto her feet. He looked up at her stormy face. "You know what I mean."

"I know that you didn't mind flirting with her."

"I wasn't flirting with Rachel, but I probably would have if I'd known it was going to make you jealous."

"I was not jealous." Joy stated through clenched teeth.

"I was jealous of Eddie DeMarco." Nick stared into her eyes.

"Quit it!" Joy put her hands over her ears.

"I can't quit it." He knew there wasn't much he could say that she'd believe. But he also knew, given enough time, he would convince her. "Sit down next to me. I won't do anything. I promise."

Joy plopped herself down at his side.

Nick put his arm around her back and laid a warm hand inside the neck of her sweatshirt. He caressed her throat.

"I'd like to tell you to go to hell, you know that?" Joy asked.

"I think you've made that point." He massaged her shoulder and the back of her neck.

Joy leaned into the touch of his fingers while she stretched her legs out next to his. She knew nothing more was going to happen between them. She expected he was thinking, as she was thinking, that any time now Diana, Kevin and her mother would be walking in.

"Will you tell me something?" Nick questioned.

"What?" Joy asked.

"Are they red?" He placed a hand lightly to her waist.

"Yes." Joy whispered the confession on a fluttering breath.

Nick shut his eyes and groaned into Joy's hair.

On that note the front door opened.

Nick and Joy barely had time to get up from the couch.

"Is it finished?" Diana asked, coming directly into the parlor with her coat still on. Kevin was right behind her.

"It is finished," Diana answered herself. "It looks terrific. Doesn't it, Kevin?"

Kevin beamed. "I told you this brother of mine knows how to paint."

"I couldn't have gotten it done without Joy." Nick smiled. "She did a lot of the work."

"I just did the molding." Joy took honest exception. "And Rachel helped."

"Rachel showed up?" Diana took off her coat and Kevin collected it. "I meant to tell you that she said she might come by to give you both a hand. Was she here for long?"

"All day," Nick said.

From behind Diana, Kevin gave Nick a look. The look Nick gave Kevin back made it resoundingly clear just how thrilled Nick had been to have Rachel around for the entire day.

"Nick," Diana said timorously. "I feel terrible about the way I behaved. Kevin told me again that you were only trying to help Eddie out. Thank you for doing the painting. I was being ridiculous thinking you were trying to ruin our wedding. Will you accept my apology?"

"Accepted," Nick smiled.

Diana threw her arms around Joy. "You are the best sister there is."

"So are you." Joy hugged back, her heart dancing that Diana wasn't accusing Nick any longer of trying to deliberately ruin the wedding.

"What do you think, Mom?" Joy asked, as her mother came into the room.

"It looks wonderful. I, for one, am delighted the painting is finished. Have you and Nick had dinner?"

"No," Joy answered, her stomach suddenly reminding her of that neglect.

"We'll grab something out," Nick said.

"Nonsense," Emily Mackey admonished. "There's enough food here to feed an army. The two of you go upstairs and shower. I'll put dinner together."

Not waiting for any rebuttal, the older woman went off to the kitchen.

"I'll go up with you," Diana said to Joy. "I feel like a load has been lifted off my shoulders." Diana gave a puckish smile. "I never did get around to telling Eddie that I wasn't going to use him to provide the music. Oh, and we've decided what songs we want played. I'll tell you upstairs."

His attention still focused on Joy's exit from the room, Nick almost missed his brother's words.

"A movie didn't cut it," Kevin said.

"I already guessed as much," Nick retorted.

"Nick," Kevin called out as Nick started to leave.

"Yeah?" Nick turned back.

"The handle for the cold water is on the right," Kevin quipped.

"Cute, Kev." Nick grinned. "But don't give up your day job."

Chapter Seven

"Do you want to play cards?" Joy asked, sitting alone with Nick in the kitchen. They'd had their late dinner and cleaned up together.

"Okay," Nick answered. He wanted to kiss her like crazy, but that hadn't been the offer.

Joy rose from the table and got out a deck from one of the kitchen drawers. She sat back down, removed the cards from their box and began to shuffle. "Poker?" she asked.

"Strip?" Nick teased.

"Doesn't anything stop you?" Joy asked sassily. "My mother is right upstairs watching TV. And Diana and Kevin could come back anytime from their ride."

Nick leaned back in his chair. "I'd rather be serious with you, but that doesn't seem to get me anywhere." There wasn't any humor on his face now.

Swallowing repeatedly, Joy shuffled the deck again. The cards fell out of her hands. Just breathing had suddenly become difficult.

Nick gathered them up. "Do you want to play with five cards or seven?"

"Five, I guess." Joy fixed her gaze on the table and chewed on the side of her mouth.

"Are you afraid to be serious with me?" Nick asked, dealing out the cards.

"Why should I be afraid?" Joy picked up the cards he'd dealt her and looked them over.

"You tell me." Nick picked up his cards, but didn't look at them.

"I have been serious with you." Joy tried getting her emotions into a state of equilibrium. "Doesn't kissing and touching count as serious?"

"It counts as being sexual, but there's more to love than sex." Nick waited a beat. "And this is a guy talking."

Joy nodded her head, which didn't give Nick any insight into what she was thinking.

"What did you feel when you first met Diana?" Joy asked.

"Hormones ... sexual attraction," Nick responded.

"Then you fell in love with her?" Joy fiddled with a button on her muted yellow-and-gray-plaid shirt, not opening it, just turning it as much as it would turn.

"I thought I did," Nick answered.

"Do you think you're in love every time your hormones act up?" Joy placed the cards she was holding down on the table.

"You ask very hard questions." He put down the cards he was holding, as well.

"I do in-depth interviews. Remember?"

Nick waited briefly, before saying, "Making a mistake about being in love happens to everyone. Haven't you ever thought you were in love, then realized you weren't?"

"Yes." Joy turned her eyes aside, then back again at him.

Nick's gaze wasn't budging. "What made you realize you hadn't been really in love?"

"He told me that I wasn't really in love with him." Joy returned her gaze to his, then looked away again. "Actually, there was someone else he was interested in making a play for, and what he was trying to do was get me to end it so he could still feel good about himself. We had been talking about marriage. I thought we would get married."

"Did you end it?" Nick asked softly. He knew the guy she was talking about was the guy she'd gone with back in college.

"Yes, but I didn't know then that he was already eyeing someone else." Joy made circles on the table with her thumb. "It took me some time to figure out he was right to begin with. I wasn't really in love with him." What it had really taken was Nick coming into her life and emblazoning himself on her heart to show her what true love was.

"I'm glad you weren't really in love with him," Nick whispered.

Joy's thumb stopped moving. "Everyone I know wants love to be easy. And the thing is, it does seem to be easy for everyone except me."

"It doesn't have to be hard," Nick responded carefully, sensing this night was a turning point for them.

"I haven't wanted to get close to anybody for a long while now."

"And now?" Nick asked, his voice low, persuasive.

The question made Joy more miserable than ever. "Why did you tell Kevin you were trying to help Eddie out when you told me that wasn't what you were doing?" She brought up the issue that had been bothering her for hours now.

"Kevin knows the real reason why I did it. He guessed even before I had a chance to tell him." The need to get her to believe him made the blood pound in Nick's head.

"I wanted Eddie away from you. I was a basket case, thinking about you going out with him again. That's the truth. You can see how that fits in with what I've been telling you, can't you?" Please, baby, see it, Nick prayed.

"I can see it possibly fitting in." Joy clutched the same button on her shirt that she'd toyed with before. She opened it and closed it. "I can also see it fitting in if you're trying to get to Diana through me."

Nick's heart hit his throat. "What do I have to say to get you to believe me?"

Joy dropped her gaze. "There's a whole lot pointing in the opposite direction. Facts are the facts."

"Facts," Nick repeated, thunderstruck. "What facts?"

Everyone of those facts flooded back to Joy, redoubling her apprehension of how gullible she could be around him.

"You want the facts, I'll give you the facts." Joy's displeasure with herself swirled out of control. "You hear that Kevin is about to marry Diana and you come back lickety-split. But you don't just come back. You come back and settle down. Correct me if I'm wrong, but that was the issue that broke you and Diana up to begin with. Then you ask Diana to go out with you when Eddie asked me to go with him to Gillie's. Let me tell you, that was a real smooth move. Which brings us to Eddie DeMarco and the reason he couldn't finish the painting..."

Joy drew a deep breath before going on. "Let's not forget the fact that you've been making a play for me, and that certainly could be to make Diana jealous."

"Why can't I be making a play for you because I'm in love with you?" He watched that stubborn chin of hers come up. "Can't you even believe that's a possibility?"

"I'll concede that it's a possibility. A small possibility," Joy said, desperately trying to hang on to her anger.

"You want to go through the facts, let's go through the facts," Nick muttered. "I've already told you that I wasn't going to come back until after Diana and Kevin were married. And right now I wish I had waited. But the paper came up for sale, and I couldn't wait on that. You know, you've never asked me how I even knew the paper was for sale. That's a fact you've missed."

"How did you know?" Joy questioned.

"I had gotten in touch with Earl right after I left East Hampton. I told him I'd keep him informed about my whereabouts so that he could send me the

JAYNE ADDISON   119

paper. I wanted to keep up with your column. Right after Kevin called me about the wedding, I heard from Earl. He asked me if I had any interest in buying the paper before he put it on the market. I came back to solidify the deal before he took it elsewhere.''

"Just like that you decided that *now* was the time to settle down?" Joy scoffed, but there was another voice in her head—a vulnerable voice saying, Hey, he wanted to keep up with your column.

"I think I made that decision the morning I kissed you on the beach and you kissed me back. Only it didn't register then.'' He assiduously avoided her sarcasm. "That kiss was fireworks. It's fireworks every time I kiss you. And don't lie to me. You feel it, too. I'll tell you something else. I feel fireworks just looking at you. I even feel fireworks when you come at me with both your barrels raised.''

"You took advantage of Kevin not being around and asked Diana out." Joy grabbed for a hook.

"I wasn't going to let you take off alone with Eddie,'' Nick answered, continuing to match her point for point.

Joy brought her eyes to his unwavering study in blue. The silence stretched, enclosing her momentarily. Then, without moving a muscle, she asked, "Are you trying to get Diana back?''

"No.'' Nick's answer was empathic. "I'm out to get you.''

Joy placed her hands on top of the table. Nick reached across to touch the tips of her fingers with his own.

She suddenly withdrew her hands and got up from the table. "I need to think.'' Even if she believed him—and she couldn't have said at that moment if she did or not—she didn't want to be someone he latched on to on the rebound. Was second best the way he saw her?

"Do you want something more to eat?" she asked stupidly, not knowing what to do or say now.

"No." Nick shuffled the deck without realizing he even had the cards in his hands. "Are you still hungry?"

"No." Joy looked at her feet. "I don't feel like playing cards anymore."

"Neither do I." Nick laid the deck of cards down. "Are you tired?"

"A little, but I couldn't fall asleep yet." She was much too unsettled to even consider it. "Would you like some music?"

"All right." He followed her with his eyes as she went over to the radio on the counter next to the stove. Eric Clapton came across the wire singing, "Knockin' on Heaven's Door." Nick couldn't have picked a better song that mirrored his thoughts.

"Dance with me," Joy invited on impulse, as his gaze connected with hers.

Nick didn't have to be invited twice. But as he got in front of her and went to draw her in, Joy quickly stepped aside.

"Are you trying to tease me?" He moved to the music with her without making another try to touch.

"You're the tease." Joy's hips swayed while her heart battered wildly. "I'm the one that's mixed up."

"Let me get you unmixed up." Nick sexily bit down on his bottom lip and raised a brow.

"I don't know if you can." Joy flipped her wild mane of cinnamon brown hair and smiled at him.

"You are one cruel woman." Nick whistled through his teeth.

"Do I really affect you?" Joy asked. She wanted him to tell her he loved her again, but she didn't know how to ask. And, she knew she still wouldn't be able to accept it even if he did say it.

"I'll play with you, if you want," Nick grinned. "But don't tell me that you don't know just how much you affect me. I haven't been able to keep it a secret when I've been kissing you. Do you know what it's like for a guy to have barely any willpower at all?"

"I know what it's like for a woman," Joy answered, rotating her hips.

"Tell me?" Nick asked.

"Just dance," Joy ordered.

"Do I get to hold you?"

"No." Joy spun around.

Nick saw a smile on her lips when she turned again to him, and he felt his chest expand with warmth. He didn't touch her—not with his hands. He touched her with his eyes.

Eric Clapton finished singing and The Rolling Stones took over. Joy suspended her motion as the even sexier, more raucous tune filled the room, but the expression she gave him was vixenish.

"I'm game, if you are," he said.

Not pulling her eyes from his, Joy let the Stones direct the heated rhythm of her body. But it was Nick Tremain's dancing, not Mick Jagger's voice, that fanned the fire that had her burning up.

Joy was winded and her hair was flying all over the place as she whirled in a final spin before coming to a halt in front of the counter as the song ended. Nick pressed his palms flat to the counter, keeping her in his space. Exhausted physically and mentally, Joy dropped her head to his shoulder. Nick buried his face in her hair. The music, which had gotten softer in the background, didn't intrude on them at all.

"Mick Jagger is Eddie DeMarco's idol," Joy said pointlessly.

"Is he?" Nick put one hand around her.

"Yes." Joy nodded her head into his shoulder. "I didn't want to go out with Eddie tonight. I didn't want to be with Eddie even when you and Diana came with us to Gillie's."

Nick put his other hand under her chin and raised her face. "Are you saying I was jealous for nothing?"

"Nick..." Joy murmured. "I really am mixed up."

"I know, baby." He hugged her gently with only that single hand around her waist. "You just keep thinking."

Joy put her arms up to his shoulders and rested them there without letting her hands curve around his neck. "You're going to make a real mark when the *East End Journal* comes out," she said softly.

"*We're* going to make a mark," Nick corrected, gazing into the bright lights in her eyes. "You and everyone else on the staff."

"It's smart of you to wait two more weeks before we put our maiden issue out." Joy's eyes stayed on him, and her heart felt as if it had dropped the burden it had been carrying—if only for that moment.

Nick's mouth edged up to a grin. "Cross your fingers that the readership loves it."

Joy crossed her fingers. Since he couldn't see them, and she didn't want to take her arms down from his shoulders, she trained her gaze on her nose and made an attempt to cross her eyes as well.

Nick laughed. "Now that's a face only a guy in love with you could love."

"Nick . . ." Joy tensed just a little.

The sound of her anxiousness made Nick's heart lurch. "I won't say it again until you're all thought out. How about that's a face only a mother could love?"

"Now that's the truth," Joy replied with a laugh.

"I'm hoping to be able to add profit sharing in six months." He strove not to say anything else that could make her uptight.

"That's going to make a lot of people happy."

The smile on her face made Nick happy. "What do you say to going house hunting with me tomorrow?"

"I'd like to."

Nick remembered he'd promised Kevin to include Diana in the project. It wasn't a promise he was glad he'd made.

"Do you mind if I ask Diana and Kevin to come along?" He minded even if she didn't, but he was stuck with it.

"Kevin doesn't usually show up on Sunday until late afternoon." Joy lost a sizable amount of her enthusiasm.

"Kevin asked me to get Diana's mind off the wedding. He's concerned she's getting herself overwhelmed. Do you mind if I still ask her to come along?"

"I don't mind." Joy did her very best not to think anything into it. "My mother might like to come, unless that would bother you." As valiantly as she tried, Joy couldn't keep herself from thinking she was going to feel like a "third wheel" if she went with just Nick and Diana.

"Absolutely, your mother." Nick hadn't liked the triangle. Emily Mackey made it better. "I can't go wrong having a woman along who knows her way around a kitchen."

"Are you insinuating I don't know my way around a kitchen?" Joy asked, feeling some relief that they weren't going to be a threesome.

"Do you?" Nick questioned teasingly.

"Not as well as my mother, but certainly better than Diana. My sister doesn't put out dinner without a phone. She doesn't even have to use her last name when she calls in an order."

Nick grinned.

Joy thought about what she'd just said. "I didn't mean for that to come out the way it sounded."

"It sounded to me like amused affection." Nick quickly gave her his opinion. "I know how much you love Diana."

Joy sighed deeply. "When we were young and we shared a bedroom, we'd put our hands out to each other before we went to sleep and we'd say, 'Don't let the bedbugs bite.' I don't know why we said that. Of course, there weren't any bugs. We just said it. I think it meant I love you."

Nick smiled tenderly at her reminiscing, but it wasn't Diana he wanted to talk about. "About your cooking... You're going to have to prove your skills to me, if you want me to believe you."

"You're on," Joy smiled. "I will cook you dinner one night."

"How about the first night I move into my new place?" If he had his way, he'd be moving her in with him.

"All right. The night you move in," Joy agreed, a total sucker for the mischief in his very blue eyes. God! If he didn't get her one way, he got her another. "We're going to have to start out first thing in the morning if we're going to accomplish any house hunting. I know Diana and Kevin made early dinner reservations for all of us. You haven't forgotten, have you? We get to debate the wedding menu tomorrow."

"Right." Nick nodded his head though he had forgotten.

"I just realized Ms. Louella didn't call today." Joy's hands came together around Nick's neck while her mind was on Diana's turmoil over the shortening of the train on her wedding gown.

"She called while you were out getting more paint with Rachel. I gave her Diana's message."

"You did?"

"Uh-huh."

"I was jealous of Rachel today," Joy confessed in a whisper as her mind skittered off Diana's wedding gown.

Nick's eyes turned an even more brilliant blue. "Not half as jealous as I was over Eddie DeMarco."

Nick held his breath then, hoping he wasn't going to turn her away by opening his heart again.

"Rachel is my best friend. That makes it worse," Joy insisted, trying to decide if she believed him while her fingers drifted into his hair.

Nick shook his head, barely. He was well aware of where her fingers were and he didn't want to dislodge them. "You didn't go to the lengths I went to." He winked at her.

"I did what I had to do," Joy said with her eyes tantalizing him. "I made sure you and Rachel didn't get an opportunity to be alone together."

"Nothing would have happened." Nick grinned, feeling on top of the world that she hadn't disputed his admission of jealousy this time. "I'm just a wolf around you."

"And a bull," Joy bantered, letting the playfulness between them carry her.

Nick groaned prankishly.

She moved out from the light hold of his embrace before she said, "I'm going to bed now."

"Sure," Nick quipped. "Now that you've killed my night's sleep. Will you at least think about me before you nod off?"

"Maybe," Joy parried. *Could she think of anything else?*

"Joy."

His voice stopped her. "Yes?"

"Don't let the bedbugs bite," Nick whispered.

"I still say the second house we went to is the one you should rent," Diana insisted, as they all sat around the kitchen table. They'd returned from house hunting and dinner at the caterer's restaurant an hour ago.

"I liked the third house we saw best," Joy refuted.

"The owner didn't do a thing to that house." Diana made a face. "How can you compare that to a house where the kitchen and bathrooms have been redone?"

"They should have been done in keeping with the Victorian charm of the house," Joy countered. "Nick can always have the bathrooms and kitchen redone if he decides to buy later on."

Diana turned her head to Kevin. "Have Nick show you both houses. I can see the one I'm talking about all decorated in my mind."

"Sweetheart," Kevin said with a smile, "let's go back to talking over the wedding menu and let Nick figure out which house he wants for himself."

"You're right, sweetheart," Diana answered distractedly. "But let's just settle this first. Nick, which house did you like better? The second one or the third one?"

"Nick might want to see a few more houses before he decides," Emily Mackey broke in diplomatically.

"I probably should see a few more," Nick responded absently. He was more concerned with the discomfort he was feeling in his stomach than which home he'd preferred.

"My vote is still on the lemon-mustard chicken," Kevin said, redirecting the flow of the conversation to the array of food they'd so recently sampled. "And I'm adding the cracked crab in butter sauce. Put those both on the buffet and I'm happy."

"The black mushroom tomato sauce with sausages," Joy said. "I don't know how I missed trying that before. You tasted it and liked it, too, didn't you, Nick?"

"Uh-huh." He had liked the dish when he'd tasted it but he wasn't so sure now.

"I still say Swedish meatballs go a long way." Emily Mackey spoke with the voice of wisdom.

"Mom is right," Diana smiled. "The Swedish meatballs, for sure. Nick, what did you think of the cold shrimp with 'green' mayonnaise?"

Nick felt himself turning as green as the shrimp dish he'd had. "I hate to break this to you. But you'd better get another caterer. I think I may have gotten food poisoning." Nick put a hand to his stomach.

"Kevin, he's doing it again!" came Diana's hysterical outpour. "How can you have food poisoning when none of us are having a problem? I'm not sick. Kevin, are you sick? Joy? Mom?"

"I am not trying to ruin your wedding," Nick insisted, getting as angry as he could, considering there was a steamroller riding over his guts.

"It could be something else," Joy said frantically. "Your appendix... Oh, my gosh!"

"His appendix came out when he was ten years old," Kevin said, looking torn between Diana and Nick.

Nick could just imagine the doubt plaguing Joy's mind. Where the hell was his luck? How could he be the only one to get sick? "It's the food. Joy, you've got to believe me. I won't eat at the wedding. Will that settle it?"

"No, that won't settle it," Diana stormed. "Nick, if you're faking this, I'm going to kill you. And I'm going to have Kevin kill you!"

"Diana," Emily Mackey reprimanded severely. "Stop it right now."

"I'm taking him to the hospital," Joy said decisively, already on her feet.

"We'll all go," Diana said.

Half an hour later they had their answer.

"He's had a reaction to shellfish," the doctor explained to the party of four in the Emergency waiting room. "I've given him a shot and a prescription he can fill tomorrow. Give him a couple of minutes for the shot to take and he can leave."

"Can I go see him?" Joy asked, her heart finally returning to its normal pace.

"Just give him a minute," the doctor responded, already stepping away.

"I feel terrible," Diana said, sinking back down into a couch. "Hold it a second ... Does he know he gets a reaction to shellfish?"

"Sweetheart," Kevin said patiently. "Nick would not make himself intentionally sick."

"You're right," Diana acquiesced as Joy took off for the treatment area.

"Nick Tremain?" Joy asked, inquiring directions at the nurses' station beyond the waiting room.

"The fourth door down." One of two nurses behind the desk pointed the way.

"Bet he's married," Joy heard behind her back.

"The gorgeous ones always are," the other nurse concluded.

"You've made a hit with the nurses," Joy said, walking into the room where Nick was resting, his hands behind his head, his chest bare. The white shirt he'd worn to dinner was tossed onto a chair.

"Come here." Nick took one hand out from behind his head to pat the side of the bed.

Joy sat where he'd indicated. She wanted to run her hands across his chest and tell him she loved him.

"Diana's sorry," she said.

He wanted to ask her if she was positive in her mind that he hadn't tried to put a chink in the wedding. "So you liked the third house we saw?" he asked instead.

"Yes," Joy answered.

Nick smiled. "My choice, too."

Chapter Eight

"Lie down with me," Nick coaxed. "Please."

It was a few days after Nick's bad reaction to shellfish and Joy had agreed to accompany him on his furniture shopping spree. But she wasn't about to agree to his proposition. "No," Joy answered resolutely, glancing again at the bed on the display room floor.

"You are difficult." He eyed her with a rapscallion grin.

"Nick . . ." Joy squealed in shock as Nick lifted her off her feet. "Will you put me down? Everyone in the store is looking at us!"

"I'm not buying a bed without testing it out." Nick tumbled Joy onto the bed and quickly stretched out next to her. "Bounce a little. No, bounce a lot."

"I am not going to bounce a little—or a lot," Joy said upbraiding him, but she was laughing.

"How are we going to know if these springs are going to hold up?"

"Will you behave yourself!" Joy went to sit up, but Nick's arm came down over her shoulders, keeping her pinned in place and giggling.

A bespectacled salesman in his late fifties approached. "Can I be of any help?"

Nick gave a theatrical performance of a guy harassed. "She is a handful. Sees a bed and she doesn't care where we are."

Joy sprang to her feet as Nick released her. "This man accosted me in the store. I don't even know him." Joy's eyes mirthfully flashed to Nick as they stood opposite each other with the king-size bed between them.

"Will you tell the nice man you're lying, before you get me arrested." Nick smiled. "See that little tick by her eye. She always gets it when she's lying. And sometimes after I've kissed her."

"I do not get a tick," Joy stated, but she felt around her eyes to be sure.

"You had a tick by your eye the first time I kissed you."

"I did not," Joy said, though she did remember trembling.

"Yes, you did." Nick stood his ground.

The salesman was following along, his head going back and forth between Joy and Nick as if he were watching a tennis match.

"That tick of yours is the cutest thing I've ever seen."

"Is it?" Joy's cheeks got pink.

The salesman cleared his throat. "If you decide on something, just call me over."

"We've decided," Nick said, before the man got away. "This is the set she likes best. I'll take it." He'd also chosen the house she'd liked best. It was the third house they'd seen the day they'd gone looking with Diana.

The salesman took a pad and pen from the pocket of his shirt and began writing. "There's a ten-day delivery," he said.

Nick picked a credit card out of his wallet and handed it over. The salesman walked off to the counter to ring up the sale.

"How do you know I like this bedroom suite best?" Joy asked. "I haven't commented about any of them."

"I saw it in your eyes." Nick gave Joy a knowing look.

"You really should have brought Diana along. She's so much better at decorating. She can picture it all in her head. I can't. What if this set is too big for the room?" His wanting to please her taste thrilled Joy while at the same time it made her crazy.

"If it doesn't fit right, I'll take a piece out and put it in another room. Okay?"

Joy punched Nick's arm. "You gave that salesman the impression we're lovers."

"We are." Nick quirked a seductive smile. "Even if it's still just in name only."

Joy scooted away from him rather than tackle that comment. "Are we going to look at furniture for the rest of the house?" she asked instead.

"Just housewares for now and we can call it a day."

"Housewares?" Joy asked, strolling with Nick to the cash register as their salesman motioned them over.

"Pots, pans, dishes, silverware, glasses. Oh, and a blanket. Where would they have blankets?"

Joy was taking notice of a suspicious look in his blue eyes. "What do you need a blanket for now? You won't have the bedroom set for ten days."

"We need a blanket for the picnic we're having tonight. I want that meal you've been promising me, even if I'm not officially moving in yet. Can't wait any longer, babe," he said, grinning into her eyes.

"What am I supposed to cook?" Her voice cracked and she cleared her throat. She didn't need him to tell her that a meal wasn't all he was after.

"Steaks. Baked potatoes. Salad, which I will cut up for you. I've already shopped and its all just waiting for your special touch." He'd purchased everything he could think of to make the meal complete, including a bottle of wine.

"Uh-huh," was all Joy could think to say, as Nick handed the signed charge slip over and received his copy. There was little she could do to combat him.

They unpacked together in the kitchen of Nick's new home, putting away everything they'd purchased that day except what they were going to need for their meal. Nick had signed the lease on the house just a few days ago. And, as he had discussed with Joy, he had indeed selected house number three—the Victorian.

"Mmm," Nick murmured, stealing a taste of marinade Joy had selected from the department store's gourmet shop. She was busily laying out the ingredients for their steak dinner.

"Will you make yourself scarce?" Joy pleaded. "I can't cook with anyone watching me." It was watching him lick his lips that had gotten to her—not that she wasn't already wildly unnerved. How long did she think she could play with fire and not get burned? *Right, Joy Mackey!* So why are you here?

"Let's have some wine first," Nick said, taking the bottle out of the refrigerator.

Joy understood now why he'd insisted on adding a set of wineglasses to his purchases. He'd neglected to mention that he already had the wine. She washed and dried two glasses, while her eyes flitted his way as he dipped a hand into the last shopping bag and brought out the blanket. The kitchen, Joy told herself, with its brightly lit fixture was hardly the place for a seduction. That thought quieted her rapid pulse some.

"Bring the glasses," Nick said, taking off with the bottle and the blanket.

"Why don't we just have the wine in the kitchen?" Joy asked nervously but trailing after him with the glasses.

Nick put the bottle down on the hardwood floor in the living room and spread the blanket out.

"Sit," he ordered.

"I'll stand." Joy's eyes skittered down to her unsteady hands holding the wineglasses. "I want to put the steaks on. You've got to be hungry. All we had for lunch was that hot dog in the mall. I know I'm starving. You must be starving. I can't believe that one hot dog has held you till now."

Nick sat down on the blanket with his eyes raised up to assess her. "Sit with me for a minute. Have a couple of sips of wine and then I'll help you get dinner on. You're not afraid of sitting down next to me, are you?"

Joy lowered herself to the blanket. She sat Indian-style with the two glasses gripped forcefully in her palms. "Is that mistletoe?" she asked, gazing upward at a sprig dangling from a dimly lit Victorian fixture above her head.

"'Tis the season," Nick grinned.

Joy scooted over to get out from being directly under the sprig.

"Too late." Nick shook his head.

"It's not too late," Joy argued, her pulse skyrocketing through the roof. How would she ever get over him if she didn't put an end to it now?

"It's too late and way too long," Nick whispered. "Do you know it's been an entire week since I've kissed you?" He pried both glasses out of her hands and put them down next to the bottle on the hardwood floor.

Joy quickly got to her feet. He looked up at her with mystified eyes. Bending at the waist, Joy plopped a kiss on his mouth and straightened back up.

He grinned at her boyishly. "Is that it? I risk life and limb to climb up a ladder that I found in the basement—and which is missing three rungs, might I add—to hang mistletoe, and that's all I get?"

"Poor baby," Joy laughed, already making a dash for the kitchen. "You should have bought a new ladder," she commented over her shoulder.

He chased after her, catching her easily. Hands to her elbows, he raised her up off her feet at the doorway to the kitchen.

"Put me down!" Joy demanded, laughing as he lifted her even higher, demonstrating his strength.

He let her down, but he didn't let go. "Kiss me right first, and I'll behave for now."

Joy put her lips to his. Keeping her mouth closed, she kissed him lightly. A fleeting smack.

"I've got to tell you, I've had better," Nick taunted, still not releasing her.

"From Diana?" Joy brought up the specter between them, though she knew perfectly well that wasn't what he'd meant.

He let go of her then. Silence ticked along for several seconds, then Nick asked quietly, "Do you really believe that?"

Joy turned away. What she believed was that she was much too near making an utter fool of herself and losing her heart forever in the bargain.

Nick's hands circled her upper arms and forced her to turn back around. "Are you using Diana to erect a barrier against me? Are you afraid to trust any guy? Is that what this is all about?"

"I—I'm afraid to trust *you*," Joy confirmed.

He watched her face, looking for a lessening in her position while he dropped his hands. "If Diana is between us, it's at your insistence, not mine."

Joy's determined gaze met his. "I know if Diana decides she wants you instead of Kevin that will be it for me." All she had to do was look in a mirror to evaluate that she wasn't any competition.

The hair bristled at the back of Nick's neck, and his shoulders tensed. "Do you realize you're not giving me a way to prove myself to you? What happens after Diana and Kevin get married? Am I off the hook then?"

"I don't want to be second-best," Joy said belligerently.

"You are hardly second-best," Nick returned tightly. "If you don't know that, if you can't feel it, then I can't show it to you or say it to you in any better way than I already have." Nick jammed his hand through his hair. "I'll cut up the salad. You can put on the steaks. If you'd rather, I can put the steaks on, as well."

"Nick..." Joy said shakily as he started to walk into the kitchen. She really didn't want to push him away. She kept doing it, but she didn't want to.

He came right back to her, the anger in his blue eyes falling away with amazing speed, to be replaced by gentle sensitivity.

"I don't know how to reach you," Nick groaned. "Do you know that?"

Joy's head bobbed up and down. Her bottom lip was quivering. "Could we just start this evening again?"

A smile wiped the pained expression off his face. "How about one more little kiss to bring peace back between us?" He brought his head down to place his mouth within easy kissing reach.

Giving him more than the price he asked, Joy put her arms around his neck and kissed him with all the feeling inside of her, taking from him everything he gave back.

Nick smiled as their lips parted. "Now that's a kiss. Are you sure you want dinner?"

"Yes," Joy lied sprightly.

He gave her a suggestive head-to-toe scan. "I don't know how I'm going to do it, but I'm going to make a believer out of you yet."

Joy raised a tentative hand and ran a finger across his mouth. "Keep trying, okay?"

"Okay." Nick winked. "Now put those steaks on, woman, before I find that finger of yours too tempting."

He hustled her into the kitchen before he could change his mind and lead her back to the blanket. "You know that expression about food being the way to a man's heart? Does it work for women?"

"No," Joy laughed, giddy and loose again.

"Give me time," Nick grinned.

Joy smirked impishly, while in her head she prayed, *Please let this be for real.*

They worked together in companionable silence. Nick took care of the salad while Joy put the potatoes in the microwave and started preparing the steaks.

Nick nearly sliced his finger open, so intent on enjoying the sight of Joy being domestic that he'd let his attention wonder from the task he was performing.

"How do you like your steak?" Joy asked, finding his blue eyes already on her.

"Still pink inside."

"Me, too."

"Sour cream or butter for your potatoes?" he asked.

"Sour cream," Joy answered.

"Me, too," Nick said.

And for no reason either could imagine, that made them both laugh.

"What about salad dressing?" Joy still had a smile on her mouth.

Nick took out an oil and balsamic vinegar dressing from a cabinet above.

"Mmm," Joy murmured. "I think I'll give that a try."

Smiling, Nick put the dressing on the counter. "Do you know you send shivers through me with that 'mmm' of yours?"

Joy rejoined, "You sent shivers through me when you said 'Mmm' before."

"Mmm," Nick murmured, giving it his best.

"Mmm," Joy whispered back, trying to outdo him.

And again they both laughed.

It took no time at all for their dinner to be ready. They took their plates and bowls into the living room. Nick put his dinner down on the blanket and went back to the kitchen for silverware. Joy looked at the two as-yet-unused glasses and the bottle of wine. She gazed up at the sprig of mistletoe.

Nick came back with silverware and napkins and a can of soda, as well. "We don't have to drink the wine."

"I'd rather have the wine," Joy said, her voice almost a whisper.

But she drank only half a glass to the two he had while they clumsily worked at cutting their meat in the plates set on their laps.

"Next meal we have at a table," Nick grinned, breaking the tension that had crept back in.

Joy ate ravenously, though Nick finished his steak, potato and salad way before she did. He took the plate and bowl from her and set it next to his.

"More wine?" Nick raised the bottle, wishing he'd thought to purchase a stereo system. A tape deck. A radio.

Joy shook her head.

Nick smiled. "Can't get you inebriated, huh?"

"No." She matched his smile.

He put the bottle down, not really wanting any more himself.

"Nick..." She wasn't looking directly at him as he lay there, stretched out and braced up on an elbow, while she sat with her feet curled up beneath her.

He heard the questioning tone in her voice. "If you want to ask me something, Joy, just ask."

"Did you know that you had an allergy to shellfish?" Joy hated asking, but it was there in her head, though she'd managed until now to keep it squelched.

"No," he replied somewhat impatiently before continuing in a calmer tone. "I haven't had shellfish for quite some time. I didn't have an allergy to it before now." He glanced at her arms, crossed defensively over her breasts. "Can you try to believe me?"

Joy nodded her head jerkily.

"Are you warm?" he asked offhandedly, springing to his feet. "I set the thermostat all the way up this morning. I haven't adjusted it at all."

"Yes." She saw the sheen of perspiration on his face and could feel the same on her own. Only it wasn't just the heating system that had caused her to grow warm.

"You can take off your sweater if you want," Joy said, trying to sound impersonal as he went to adjust the thermostat.

He sat back down next to her and ran a hand randomly through his hair. "I couldn't possibly consider making myself more comfortable unless you're going to do the same."

Joy laughed, knowing from his teasing that he'd forgiven her for asking him about the shellfish. "What would you do if I took you up on that?"

"I could sit on my hands if you want." He reached out to tentatively brush her breast.

Joy removed his hand and held it down on the floor. "We're just talking about it as a possibility." It was all she could do to keep a straight face. It was all she could do to keep from moaning.

Nick dropped his head down to the blanket and used his other hand to circle the back of her neck. "You're still under the mistletoe," he whispered, before he pulled her down and captured her mouth.

Joy flattened herself on top of him while they both made sounds of frustrated passion. Suns and moons and every other excuse she'd ever come up with to explain her reaction to him flashed across her mind as she let her tongue and lips and hands respond to him. They were pressed together so tightly that not even a bedbug could have come between them.

The doorbell did that, jarring them both.

"Who the hell could that be?" Nick growled, letting the ring continue.

"I think you'd better go see." Joy drew a deep, shuddering breath as she rolled off him. "Your car is

in the driveway. Whoever it is will know that someone is home.''

He kissed her again, quickly, before he got up and
went to the front door.

"Hi," Diana and Kevin chimed as Nick opened the
door.

Diana went on blithely. "Before she left for her
weekend with her friends, Mom told me that you and
Joy were having dinner here. We brought cake for
dessert. We just had the worst meal ever. I'm absolutely certain now that we've picked the right caterer."

"Diana insisted we come over," Kevin said with just
enough of an apology in his voice for Nick to pick up
on.

Diana had already entered the house, and by the
time the brothers caught up, she had handed Joy the
cake box and was unbuttoning her coat.

"Where can we put our coats?" Diana asked Nick
as Kevin was slowly removing his.

Back on, was the immediate response Nick had in
his head.

"There are hangers in the closet," Joy answered.
"I'll take them from you. Here, hold the cake."

"Black Forest," Diana enthused with the box back
in her hand.

Nick didn't try for an eager expression or even a
polite one. Diana didn't notice. She was eyeing the
dinner plates and bowls still on the floor.

Joy returned and Diana said to her, "I'll help you
clean up. Then we can have the cake. I'm glad I'm
wearing slacks. I didn't think about there not being a

table and chairs. Oh, Nick, why don't you show Kevin around.''

It wasn't until Diana and Joy were alone in the kitchen that Diana took a closer look at Joy.

"Is something going on between you and Nick?'' her sister asked.

"Going on?'' Joy repeated, as she scraped off their dinner dishes.

"Have you and Nick gotten personally involved?'' Diana put it more pointedly.

"Would it bother you if we were?'' Joy returned, ruthlessly scrubbing the frying pan with a sponge she'd drenched in dishwashing liquid.

Diana contemplated. "I think it would.''

"Why?'' Joy placed the clean frying pan on the counter and began attacking the dishes. "You wanted to fix Nick up with Rachel.''

"That's different,'' Diana answered dismissively. "Is there a towel?''

"Paper towels,'' Joy responded. "Why would it be different for Nick to be involved with Rachel?''

"It just would be. And you do work with him, that could be tricky.'' Diana unwound a wad of paper towels and began wiping the pan. "You haven't fallen for him, have you?''

"No,'' Joy lied, feeling as if Eddie DeMarco's prediction had come true. It was abundantly obvious that just the thought of Nick being interested in her had Diana jealous.

"Do you have small plates for the cake?'' Diana asked.

"Yes.'' Joy sluggishly nodded.

"How about coffee?''

"No," Joy answered listlessly.

Diana walked to the doorway of the kitchen. "Kevin," she called.

"Yes," Kevin answered the summons, coming down from the second floor with Nick.

"Would you and Nick go out and get us all coffee? I think there's a deli just down the street."

"Do you want me to see if I can find someplace to get cappuccino?" Kevin asked.

"Regular coffee is fine for me." Diana turned her head to Joy. "Would you rather cappuccino if Kevin can find a place?"

"No," Joy said indifferently. She didn't care what she drank. Her life was over.

"Joy, will you come with me tomorrow to pick up my wedding gown?" Diana asked a little while later as the two couples sat around finishing their dessert.

"Sure," Joy answered. She'd barely spoken at all since Kevin had returned with coffee. And when she had, it had only been to respond with single syllable words. Joy didn't think her quiet was noticeable. Diana, with Kevin's smiling adoration, had been keeping up a steady chatter.

"I can't believe that the wedding is next Sunday," Diana continued. "Kevin, can you believe it?"

Kevin grinned. "It's starting to hit me."

Diana slid her smile from Kevin to Nick. "I know I'm not supposed to ask, but are you planning a surprise stag party?"

Nick felt badly that he hadn't even thought about it. "You had it right to begin with. You're not supposed to ask." He delivered the line as glibly as he could.

"Nick, if you have one in mind, cancel it," Kevin said. "I'd rather just the two of us go out for a couple of drinks."

"No problem. If that's what you want."

Diana sighed happily, then stifled a yawn. "I feel like I've been going and going forever now."

"Tired, sweetheart?" Kevin asked.

"Yes." Diana covered another yawn with her hand.

"Come on. Let's go."

At Kevin's magic words the light dawned at the end of a long tunnel for Nick.

"I'll help Joy clean up first," Diana said, getting up.

"Don't worry about it," Nick said quickly. "I'll do the dishes."

"We may as well all leave together," Joy said. "I'm tired myself."

"Sure." Nick sighed as the light at the end of the tunnel blew out. "If you're tired, you're tired."

"I am tired," Joy reaffirmed, already leading the way to the kitchen.

In a matter of minutes they were all out the front door. Nick practically had to force Joy into riding back with him instead of with Kevin and Diana.

"I know what's been wrong with me. Diana and Kevin's arrival," Nick said, starting his car while Joy sat huddled in her jacket. "What's been wrong with you?"

"Diana and Kevin's arrival," Joy answered without intonation, letting him make of it whatever he chose. She laid her head back against the seat and closed her eyes.

"Are you really that tired?"

"Yes." Joy made it sound like she meant it.

"Bull!" Nick growled as he drove.

Joy's eyes flashed open and her head came up. "What do you want me to say, Nick?"

"I want you to say you trust me. How about trying it on just for size?"

"Diana is jealous," Joy stated bluntly.

Nick needed a second with that one. "Are you saying that you told Diana about us?"

"I didn't tell her. She just suspected it."

"And you confirmed it?" The start of a smile began at one side of Nick's mouth.

"No." Joy jutted her chin out. "I denied it."

"Then Diana has no reason to feel jealous." Nick's voice held a sharp edge of frustration. "Not that she's really jealous, Joy. If anything she might be feeling a little strange at the idea. But that's it."

"Call it whatever you want." The duplicity she'd felt the last time she'd thought she was in love was fresh again in her mind.

He looked her way. "I'd like to tell you to go to hell, do you know that?"

"I believe I've already said the same to you," Joy retorted.

"All right. You said it first. I'm saying it second. We can fight about that now."

"I don't want to fight. Just . . . leave me alone."

Nick pounded the steering wheel once. "I'm not leaving you alone. You're not going to win, Joy. Because if you win, we both lose."

"Nick . . ." Joy said his name tremulously. "I got really hurt the last time I thought I was in love."

"I know, baby," Nick said achingly.

She watched him hold a hand out to her. Shiveringly, Joy put her hand to his.

"No more tonight," Joy pleaded.

"No more tonight," Nick whispered back.

Chapter Nine

The following morning Joy walked by Nick's bedroom and saw through the open door that his bed had already been made. She checked her watch again. It was just eight a.m. Not unexpectedly Diana's door was still closed.

Joy found Maxie downstairs in the front hall. The huge mutt pounced up to place his front paws happily on her shoulders.

"You wanting to go out?" Joy ran a hand over the dog's fur. "Oh, you have been out." Maxie's coat was damp. It had snowed during the night, coming down heavily enough to still be around to make it a white Christmas in ten days.

Joy heard the scrape of a shovel against asphalt. Moving the lacy beige curtain at the front door windowpane aside, she looked out to see Nick shoveling snow. Grabbing her long navy coat out of the closet she put it on along with her knit cap and gloves and went outside.

"I'll help," Joy said, calling to Nick as she came down the driveway.

Leaning his weight on the long-handled snow shovel, Nick smiled. "This is man's work."

"I have more muscles than you know," Joy answered cockily.

"Oh, yeah?" Nick's smile widened to a grin. "Come here and let me feel."

Joy gave Nick a cheeky, not-on-your-life look and went into the opened garage for another snow shovel.

"Have I ever told you that I love you in that hat?" Nick asked, as side-by-side they both pushed their shovels into a mound of snow.

"No," Joy laughed. "I can tell you for certain that I don't believe that." Her shovel came up from the driveway with a lot less snow on it than his.

"Hey," Nick said with a grin. "Are you saying that you're starting to believe some of what I've been saying? Is that a little wavering I'm hearing?"

"My brain doesn't function as well first thing in the morning as it does later on in the day." Joy flippantly dumped the snow from her shovel onto the snow-covered lawn.

"And here I thought I was smart, saving all my best stuff until the sun came down." Nick didn't just dump the snow off his shovel, he tossed the shovel, snow and all.

"What are you doing?" Joy asked wide-eyed as he pulled the shovel she was holding out of her hands.

"What do you think I'm doing?" His smile got closer and closer to her mouth. "I'm taking advantage of the hour."

It was a devouring kiss on both their parts, though they were unable to press hard enough against each other through the bulk of their clothing to satisfy either of them.

"Now what were you saying about muscles?" Nick asked, as Joy's eyes opened languorously. He put the heel of one hand to a breast, hidden from him beneath her sweater and coat.

"That's not where they are," Joy whispered impudently.

"No?" Nick kissed the hollow of her neck, while Joy's head fell back weakly.

"No..." Joy strained with arousal and the need to feel far more of his touch.

Nick raised Joy's hat just a little up from one ear and put his mouth to the lobe he'd uncovered. "Can I interest you in having breakfast over at my place this morning?"

Joy released a shaky breath as she shook her head. "I'm going with Diana to pick up her wedding gown. I'm sure she'll want to go early."

Nick's hand left the front of Joy's coat. "Is that the only reason I can't get you alone?"

"Hard question," Joy teased.

"In-depth," Nick quipped his retort.

"You know what I thought about before I fell asleep last night?" Joy asked, all humor gone from her voice.

"What did you think about?" Nick prompted at the pause, though he already knew from her tone that it wasn't going to be something he wanted to hear.

"If you had been willing to settle down months ago, you and Diana would be married by now."

Nick took a deep breath and picked his shovel up before he responded. "We would have never made it down the aisle. We would have both realized we weren't right for each other." He rammed his shovel into the snow on the driveway. "I guess the morning reprieve is over. Your brain seems to be functioning at full speed again."

Joy picked up her shovel and braced her chin on the back of a gloved hand, trying to hold on to the slim thread of necessary obstinacy she had left. There hadn't been anything at all wrong with his answer. Or his anger.

"You're right. This is man's work," Joy said, letting the shovel drop from her hand before she crossed to the lawn and began slogging through the snow toward the house. She wasn't winning this battle.

"One of these days you're going to trust me," Nick said, loading his shovel and turning it over at the side of the driveway. "I hope we're both still young enough to enjoy it."

Joy stopped in her deep tracks. She made a clumsy U-turn and faced him. "I wasn't going to bring Diana up. I told myself not to say it. I don't know how to make myself stop."

Nick groaned to himself and looked at her. Obstinate, prickly and frustrating. But he wouldn't have changed a hair on her head.

"Come back here." His voice came out in a gritty near whisper.

Joy retraced the deep steps she'd made. Her eyes were on his lingering smile.

"How about you just stand here and watch and let me show off?" he said when she picked up her shovel.

"Then I can't show off," Joy answered, reconnecting with him in the way that was easiest.

Nick grinned. "Will I bring the roof down over my head again if I say you've already wowed me? I mean the sky."

"Let me think," Joy bantered, giving a measuring look up at the sky.

"Hurry up." Nick grabbed a handful of snow, then gazed at her with fair warning in his daredevil eyes.

"If you throw snow at me, I'm going to throw snow back at you." Joy laughingly refuted his threat, backing away from him as she said it.

She ducked as a snowball went sailing over her head. The snowball she threw back hit the shoulder of Nick's leather jacket because he hadn't tried to get out of her way. But he did charge after her then. Joy took off into the snow, and he followed, finally grabbing her around the waist and holding her to him.

"I don't think you've got very much fight left in you," Nick said, as she made a petty attempt to extricate herself. "Why don't you give it up now and tell me you love me?"

"Egotist," Joy accused.

"Sticks and stones..." Nick nipped the tip of her nose.

Joy nipped his jaw, and Nick laughed deeply.

"Torture me all you want, babe." Nick's mouth turned up in a very satisfied male grin. "I'll take whatever you want to give."

"Is that so?" Joy murmured.

"That's so." Nick smiled.

Joy reached up for his head and pulled him down, initiating their kiss. Nick groaned and kissed her back. And though it didn't come near to fulfilling their needs, they pleasured each other with their mouths in a rapturous swirl of sensation, neither caring if a car happened to pass by.

"Do you have any idea what you're doing to me right now, acting free and open like this?" Nick asked against Joy's lips.

"I don't think I need all that much of a brain to figure it out," Joy parried, arms crooked around his neck, head tilted teasingly to one side.

"That, too." Nick's grin was audacious. "But I'm talking about this." He took one of her hands down from his neck and brought it inside his leather jacket. "Can you feel that?" He pressed her damp glove to his chest.

Joy felt the hammering of his heart beneath her hand through his sweater and her wool glove. The thrumming of Joy's own heart filled her ears. "Yes."

"Good..." He nibbled the corner of her lips before his kiss grew wholly demanding.

"Don't go with Diana," Nick rasped.

"I have to," Joy moaned.

"Will you come with me to my place after you finish up with Diana?" Nick asked solemnly.

"Yes," Joy answered, just as solemnly sealing her fate. *I love you, Nick Tremain. I can't help it.*

Nick reached down for some snow, balled it in his hand, threw it high up in the air and winked at her. "Now, stop breaking my concentration and let me get this driveway done."

Nick picked up his shovel. Joy picked up hers, but Nick took it away from her. "How about you go inside, get nice and warm and put on some coffee?" He was worried about her catching a cold.

"I'll help," Joy insisted.

"Believe me, I can get this done faster alone. You're too much of a distraction."

"Do you want some pancakes?" Joy asked shyly, poking the toe of a rubber boot into the snow.

"I'd love some pancakes." Nick smiled.

"You made pancakes," Diana said, as she sat down at the kitchen table dressed for the day in front-pleated oyster gray slacks and a soft sweater to match.

Nick passed Diana the platter brimming over with pancakes. He'd just sat down at the table himself with Joy. He hadn't even had a chance to say a word to her.

"I really shouldn't..." Diana vacillated. "Well, maybe I'll have just one."

Joy watched Diana select the noticeably smallest one.

At her turn, Joy piled her plate with four pancakes, though she couldn't imagine herself eating. Her stomach was quivering.

Nick helped himself to a stack of five.

Joy glommed on butter and syrup. Nick did the same.

Diana ignored the butter, but dribbled on a little syrup.

"As good as your mother's," Nick said, having already swallowed a mouthful.

"Thank you." Joy's eyes didn't meet his. She'd committed herself to sharing the most intimate of acts with this man, and there was no calming her heart down now.

"Where do you have to go to pick up your gown?" Nick asked Diana, though his eyes remained on Joy. He hadn't missed noticing that she wouldn't look him in the eye.

"East Hampton," Diana answered, pouring herself some coffee. "I've decided I'm not going to try it on again there. I'll put it on here where I can take my time and be more relaxed."

"Is Kevin coming by?" Nick asked.

"Yes." Diana nodded her head. "He'll be here in the afternoon. He's already called me this morning. He wanted to know if he's going to get to see me in my wedding gown. Which he isn't. I'm not taking any chances on bad luck. Joy, hurry and finish up. I'd like to be there when they open. Do you think they open later on Sunday than the rest of the week?"

"Their hours are probably listed on their receipt," Joy responded. "If you look in my closet the receipt for my bridesmaid's dress is still pinned to the bag."

Diana pushed the plate with her half-eaten pancake aside to fly upstairs.

Nick's eyes went from the fork Joy was just dangling in her hand to her lowered eyes. "Joy?"

"Hmm?" She braved a quick glance.

"You can change your mind." Nick drew a breath. And they both knew what he was referring to.

"I know..." Joy swallowed. His sensitivity was as wonderfully devastating to her as everything else about him.

"Do you want to change your mind?" He had time for a longer, more careful look at the apprehensive expression on her face as she raised her eyes fully to him.

"No," Joy whispered. She meant it. For all her trepidation, Joy meant it.

Diana came back into the kitchen with the receipt in her hand. "They open at eleven today. Joy, hurry and finish up. It's going to take longer to get there with the roads the way they are. We can go for a cup of coffee if they're not open when we get there."

Nick hadn't given any thought to the roads being hazardous. "I'll drive the two of you there."

Diana smiled. "You sound like Kevin. He wanted me to wait until he could get here to drive me, which would have had him making the trip back and forth and back again. My car is four-wheel drive with anti-lock brakes. I don't have a problem with driving in snow. I heard a truck come by clearing the roads, anyway."

"I'm driving," Nick said, not at all swayed. "Tell you what . . . I'll toss in lunch."

"All right." Diana smiled. "As long as it's some-place I can get a salad. I know the kind of places you two like to go to eat."

Joy picked up her dish and took it over to the garbage can by the sink.

"You didn't eat anything," Diana said, following Joy with her own dish. "Are you feeling all right? It's not like you, not to eat. Is something bothering you? Let me feel your head."

"I don't need you to feel my head. Nothing is bothering me. I'm feeling fine," Joy answered impatiently, trying not to think of herself as a "third wheel."

"Let's just leave the dishes in the sink," Diana said, as Nick brought up his dish. "We'll do them when we get back. I'm just going to run upstairs, call Kevin and get a scarf. Since we're going to be in East Hampton for lunch I'm sure Kevin will want to meet us."

A little peace settled in the corner of Joy's heart. Four was much better than three.

"We'll meet you outside," Nick called to Diana, as he went to the hall closet for their coats. He put on his jacket and held Joy's coat for her.

As she put her arms through the sleeves Joy wanted to say something to him . . . but she couldn't think of anything.

Nick turned Joy to him and started buttoning her coat. "You okay?" he whispered.

Joy nodded.

Diana was just coming down the stairs to get her coat from the hall closet as Joy and Nick went out the front door. At the side of Nick's car, Joy opened the back seat door. Nick's hand shot forward to close the back door before Joy had a chance to seat herself. He opened the passenger door.

"Don't give me any of your lip," Nick threatened with a smile.

Joy sat herself in the passenger seat. Crazy as it was, the action he'd just taken spoke louder to Joy than any of the words he'd said to her. As Nick got in on the driver's side, she scooted as close to him as she could get. Nick smiled over at her as he put the key into the ignition.

Diana got into the back. "Kevin suggested Trotto's," she said, crossing her legs. "He'll be there between twelve and twelve-fifteen."

* * *

"Two rolls. Why did you butter two rolls for me?" Diana moaned to Kevin as they all went into the house some two hours later. "If my gown doesn't fit, I'm going to murder you."

Kevin grinned. "Take your coat off. Go upstairs with Joy and try your gown on. Then we can all put our heads together and decide what to do with the rest of today."

"You two are on your own," Nick said. "Joy and I already have plans."

Nick's glance swept Joy's face. They hadn't spoken of anything personal or even kidded with each other, though they'd had the opportunity to do so when it was just the two of them returning from East Hampton. But her hand had rested on his shoulder the entire trip back.

"What plans?" Diana asked, taking her coat off.

"To do with the paper," Joy said, feeling her face flush. She wasn't ready yet to expose in any way that they were a couple. The realization had only just settled in her mind. For the moment it seemed wonderful to have it a secret just between the two of them.

"Are you going to be working here in the house?" Kevin asked innocently while Diana hung up her coat.

"No..." Joy and Nick spoke over each other.

Joy looked at Nick, and neither was able to control the size of their smiles. He saw that she'd forced her hair behind her ears to keep it from flying in her face outdoors. It was bunched against her neck where he wanted more than anything to bury his mouth.

Diana carefully took her gown from Kevin's hand. "Joy, you're not leaving before I try on my gown, are you?"

"Of course not." Joy brought her smile to Diana and began unbuttoning her coat. She took it off, handing it to Nick as he reached out for it.

Nick watched as Joy went upstairs with Diana. He unzipped his jacket but didn't take it off. He was counting on the trying-on process not taking too much time. He could barely contain his impatience to be alone with her again—whether or not they made love. What he needed most of all was to hear her say she believed him. He was certain she was finally feeling it.

"Bring me up-to-date on the paper," Kevin said, putting his coat in the closet.

"Barring anything unforeseen, we'll have the first issue out middle of next week." Nick walked along with Kevin to the kitchen.

"You've still got the *Greenport News* out there, right?"

Nick nodded his head. "Last issue."

"Want some coffee?" Kevin asked, having opened the thermos on the kitchen table to see what it contained.

Nick shook his head, remembering then the dishes from breakfast. He was about to take his jacket off and do the dishes when a shrieking scream came from upstairs.

The brothers looked at each other in bewilderment before they both made a mad dash out of the kitchen.

Diana's bedroom door was closed, which brought Kevin and Nick up short for a moment. At another shriek from inside, Nick pushed open the door.

Diana was sitting plopped on her bed in her wedding gown. It was clear immediately to the brothers that the shrieking had been coming from Diana. Her chest was still heaving.

Kevin rushed to her. "What is it, sweetheart? What's wrong?"

"What's wrong?" Diana repeated hysterically. "You want to know what's wrong? Look at me!" Diana jumped to her feet.

"I don't know how this could have happened," Joy said, all distressed.

"Do you see now?" Diana raved, looking down at herself. "How can I get married in this? It's too short!"

"You've tried it on a number of times in the store," Kevin said helplessly, but using a soothing voice. "How did it get to be too short?"

"I don't know. But I am not getting married looking like . . . like this!"

Nick saw the lines of accusation that flashed across Joy's face as she turned to look at him. He swallowed convulsively.

"Joy," Diana moaned. "When you spoke to Ms. Louella you did make it clear that it was the train I wanted shortened, not the gown . . . didn't you?"

The train, Nick thought. What the hell was the train?

"I took the call from the bridal shop." Nick stepped forward to take his punishment like a man. "Joy was out getting more paint with Rachel."

"You!" Diana's accusation was even more virulent than Joy's.

"I heard you tell Joy you wanted it shortened three inches. I thought I had it right," Nick said, growing a little irritated. "Can't you have material or something put on the bottom?"

"No...I can't have material or something put on the bottom," Diana wailed.

"Nick." Joy's articulation was tight. "I think we should step out for a minute and let Kevin be alone with Diana."

Nick made a mental note to himself that after he got himself out of his one, he was going to stay as clear of this damned wedding as he could get. Then he followed Joy out of the room.

"Joy," Nick began, as she closed the door behind them. "I did not do it on purpose. I'll pay for a new gown. Give me a break. Okay?"

Joy clasped her arms in front of her chest. "I thought your first question would be are we still going to your place."

Nick took a breath in through his teeth. "Are you that mad?"

"I'm not mad." Joy's obstinate chin came up.

"Don't hold back." Nick pushed a hand through his hair.

"All right. I'm mad. I'm mad...I'm mad at myself," Joy sputtered. "I guess I can't hold you accountable because I'm stupid. When you get down to it, I've been stupid since I met you."

"What does that mean?" Nick asked, although he thought he might be better off not asking.

"I'll tell you what it means," Joy retorted. "This morning you had me believing I could trust you—that you really were over Diana...that you weren't trying to ruin the wedding to give yourself more time for a second chance. Have you ever heard anything as stupid as that?''

"Joy," Nick begged.

Joy waved a silencing hand in the air. "Give me one of your credit cards. If I have to take Diana to every bridal shop on Long Island, she's going to get another gown. And you're paying for it."

Nick took out his wallet and removed his gold card. "I don't care what it costs. Whatever. Could you just hear me out for a second?"

"No!" Joy grabbed the card and walked back into Diana's bedroom. Nick stayed in the hallway, but he wasn't alone for long.

"Let's take this outside," Kevin said tersely, coming out of Diana's bedroom.

Nick let out an exasperated breath. "Kevin, this isn't your style."

"Well, I've got a new style." Kevin tossed this statement over his shoulder angrily as he went down the stairs, Nick trailing behind him.

Kevin yanked open the front door and stepped out.

Nick stayed put. "Get back in here, Kevin. I'm not going outside with you unless you put your coat on. You sure as hell won't be getting married with pneumonia."

That brought Kevin back inside for his coat.

"I know how you're feeling," Nick said, when they were both outside. "You need to blow off steam. Go ahead, blow off steam with me. I know how bad this looks. But I'm telling you the truth, Kevin. I did not deliberately try to mess up Diana's gown. Dammit! I can't wait for the two of you to get married."

Kevin threw a punch.

Nick sidestepped it. "Kevin, think it through. Have I made a single pass at Diana?"

"Are you saying you think she'd let you get away with anything if you tried?" Kevin balled his hand into a fist again.

Nick let out an explosive breath. "Did I stop speaking English?"

Joy and Diana came out of the house.

"Where are you going, sweetheart?" Kevin asked, as Diana and Joy walked by the two of them.

"We're going to House of Brides," Diana said, sniffling.

"Do you want me to drive you?" Kevin asked.

Diana shook her head. "I want to be with just my sister right now. Joy is going to drive."

"Go ahead and punch me now," Nick said under his breath to Kevin. "Hurry up, before they drive off."

Joy and Diana saw Kevin punch Nick in the jaw. Joy's heart jumped and her breathing ceased. Joy put her hand to the door, set to rush out of the car.

Diana got a firm hold of Joy's arm. "Joy, if you go to him, I'll never speak to you again."

Joy watched Nick steady himself. It didn't seem that he was hurt.

"Feel better now?" Nick asked Kevin as Joy backed out of the driveway.

Kevin's response was another punch. Not seeing this one coming, Nick took it once more on his jaw.

"Kevin, I'm not going to hit you back. But I'm not going to stand here and be a punching bag for you, either. You've made your point about the gown. I'm sure it made Diana feel better."

"That wasn't for the gown," Kevin answered, brandishing a fist in the air again.

This time Nick sidestepped out of the way, then got a grip on both of Kevin's wrists. "What was it for?" Nick asked.

"That was for being with Diana." Kevin pulled against Nick's grip.

"I never made love to Diana. That is what you're talking about, isn't it?"

"That's what I'm talking about." Kevin stopped trying to pull out of Nick's hold.

"Did Diana tell you we made love?" Nick asked, annoyed and aggravated that Diana was playing that kind of game.

"You don't think I'd speak to Diana about the two of you," Kevin snapped. "It's hard enough thinking about her making a comparison."

"There's nothing to compare." Nick relaxed, finally understanding. "We *never* made love. Honest to God. She'd read this article in some woman's magazine about relationships growing stronger without sex."

"You're kidding?" A faint smile started across Kevin's mouth.

"I kid you not." Nick grinned, letting go of Kevin's wrists. "I guess that article bit the dust."

Kevin's smile grew, which was answer enough.

"You know something," Nick said, ruminating. "I didn't push the issue all that much. I think my libido was telling me something my brain hadn't figured out. I'd bet you anything, now, that it was the same for Diana."

"Have you straightened things out with Joy?" Kevin asked.

Nick groaned. "This wedding gown fiasco took the cake as far as she's concerned. It kills me, but I can see how she'd think I've been trying to put a hatchet to your wedding plans. First there's Eddie and the painting. Then the shellfish. And now the gown... Oh, and let's not forget I asked Diana to go out with me because I wanted to tag along when Eddie asked Joy to go to Gillie's."

"You do seem to have racked them up. What you've got is a credibility problem."

Nick nodded his head. "I'm also freezing. Can we go inside?"

"Yes." Kevin smiled sheepishly. "I'm sorry I hit you."

Nick grinned. "Consider it justice for all the times I got you when we were kids."

"I can try talking to Joy, if you want," Kevin said when they were inside.

"How about running off with Diana to Vegas tonight? I'll pay for the tickets."

"Sorry. She's got her heart set on this wedding." Kevin hung up his coat, then gave his watch a glance. "The game's going on. How about we watch some football?"

"Yeah, why not..."

The game was in halftime when Diana and Joy returned from House of Brides.

There was a big smile on Diana's face as she burst into the TV room with her coat still on. She was carrying a wedding gown in a House of Brides plastic bag. Joy followed her into the room slowly.

"Ms. Louella got a shipment in on Friday that she hadn't even unpacked," Diana excitedly told Kevin. "We went through it together and there it was. If I had seen this gown first, it would have been the one I would have picked. And the best part is, it didn't need any alterations. Nothing..."

Nick got the import of Diana's chatter, though he was only taking in every other word. The better part of his absorption was on Joy. Her hair was ruffled just the way he'd come to expect it to look after catching the wind. She wasn't looking at him, but her expressive features no longer seemed as tense.

"Do you want to come to my bedroom and see it?" Diana said, beckoning Kevin with her eyes.

"Are you going to try it on for me?" Kevin asked, moving toward her.

"No," Diana admonished. "I've already told you that's bad luck."

Left behind, Joy put her hand in the pocket of her jeans and brought out Nick's credit card and charge slip and held it out to him. "They let me sign your name. I told Ms. Louella that she could reach you at the paper if the bank gave her a problem."

Nick got up from the armchair where he'd been sitting to take the card and slip from her. She wasn't coming forward. But she did look at him when he got near enough.

"Did Kevin hurt you?" Joy asked, trying to sound unconcerned.

Nick shook his head.

"I guess Kevin's decided to believe you."

Nick nodded. "So...ah...Diana seems happy."

"What's your point?" Joy asked archly.

"I don't have one." Nick's voice lowered to a coarse whisper. "Not a new one. Just the one I've been making to you all along."

Joy thought about walking out of the room. She thought about leaving the paper. She thought about him suing her. Could a judge force her to work out her contract?

"Are you watching the game?" she asked.

"Yeah," Nick shrugged. "Do you like football?"

"Yes," Joy answered briefly.

Nick waited several breaths. "Will you watch the game with me?"

"Okay." You're pitiful, Joy! You are truly pitiful.

Nick took a seat on the couch and Joy sat at the other end. She'd left a space—too large a space to suit Nick. He couldn't have reached her with his arm out. Still, there was less space between them now than when she'd left to go back to the bridal shop.

But Nick didn't know if he'd ever be able to eliminate the space that kept her heart apart from his.

Chapter Ten

Joy was just parking her car after a long day at work when Nick pulled in behind her. Previously she'd gone to work with him in his car, but not these past two days. It was two days since he'd ruined Diana's first wedding gown—two days since she'd been driving herself to work—two days of nothing but business between them.

Nick caught up with Joy as she started to walk to the front of the house. They were both surprised to see Kevin's car parked on the curb.

"I thought Kevin said he was definitely going to have to work through the night all this week to get his calendar squared away," Joy commented in the polite, professional voice she'd been using with Nick. She was holding the first edition of the *East End Journal*. She'd brought it home to show off. With the exception of her excitement over the paper, she'd hated every minute of the past two days.

"That's what I heard him say," Nick responded, opening the front door for Joy to step in. It was five days away from the wedding. He was counting the hours . . . the minutes.

Joy and Nick hung their coats in the closet, then proceeded to the kitchen. He let her get ahead of him just to watch her walk. If he couldn't touch her, he could at least enjoy her with his eyes.

"I wonder where everyone is," Joy said as they found themselves in an empty kitchen.

"They've got to be somewhere." Nick shrugged.

Joy put the *East End Journal* down on the kitchen table and went back to the front hall, Nick right behind her.

"Mom?" Joy called from the bottom of the stairs.

"Diana's bedroom," her mother called down.

Joy and Nick took the wide stairs together.

Emily Mackey met them in the upstairs hallway.

"Is something wrong?" Joy asked, an alarmed palm to her chest. Her mother looked very upset.

"Your sister has called off the wedding." The older woman wrung her hands. "I've talked to her till I'm blue in the face. Kevin is talking to her now, but she doesn't seem to be listening. I haven't even made dinner. The two of you must be starving. I'll get dinner started. That's what I'll do. Poor Kevin...I'm sure he hasn't had dinner."

Joy watched her mother hurry off. Then she looked at Nick with her stomach winding into a zillion knots.

Nick looked back at Joy with his gut fiercely clenched.

Together they looked at Diana's closed bedroom door.

"I'm not going to just stand here," Nick said tautly, after moments of fractured silence.

"What do you suggest we do?" Her voice wasn't any less strained than his.

Wordlessly Nick rapped on the closed bedroom door.

"Come in." It was Kevin who answered, his voice distraught.

Joy stepped in behind Nick and saw Kevin and Diana sitting side by side on Diana's bed. Kevin had his arms around Diana's compressed shoulders and her head was down.

Diana lifted her head slowly. Tears were streaming down her cheeks. "Joy..." she said in a voice broken by sobs.

"I'm here, Diana." Joy's heart went achingly out to her sister.

Nick put a hand on his brother's shoulder. "Let Joy talk to Diana alone."

Beleaguered, Kevin pulled himself up from the bed.

Nick ushered Kevin out of the room, pulling the door shut behind them.

Kevin stared at the closed door as he stood in the hallway with Nick.

"What happened?" Nick asked compassionately.

"I don't know." Kevin pressed his hand to his eyes. "She wouldn't tell me. She said she just didn't want to get married."

"Let me take you out for a drink," Nick said, trying to do something to help.

"I need to get out," Kevin told him, agonized. "But alone. I want to be alone."

Nick was scared; he'd never seen his brother this upset. "I don't want you driving. Take a walk. Okay?"

"Leave me be, Nick." Kevin turned toward the stairs.

Nick quickly moved in front of his brother. "You're not going anywhere unless you give me your keys. Don't make me knock you around."

"You want the keys..." Kevin yanked them out of his pocket. "Here's the keys." He threw them down.

Nick moved aside and Kevin walked to the stairs.

"Do you think you can talk now?" Joy asked gently, as Diana's sobs turned to soundless spasms. She was rocking Diana in her arms, having taken Kevin's place at Diana's side.

"How... how does anyone kn-know if they're going t-to be in love for a li-lifetime?"

Joy grabbed a handful of tissues from a box on the bed. She tenderly wiped Diana's face.

"You just know," Joy said, her throat clogged with emotion.

"I don't know," Diana babbled, mindlessly. "Sometimes I think it's all just a bunch of words. He says he loves me. I say that I love him. How do I know he's going to stay in love with me? How do I know he's really in love with me now? He could just *think* he's in love with me."

Joy's voice quavered as she whispered, "When someone loves you, you just know it with your heart." It was a truth that had eluded Joy until she'd said it.

She hadn't let herself listen to Nick with her heart. She'd thought she knew everything. She'd thought she had it all figured out.

Diana dropped her head. "I can't get married feeling like this. Maybe we don't belong together. Maybe I'm not supposed to marry him. Maybe I'm supposed to marry someone else. If I'd married Nick, then Kevin and I wouldn't be together now. Maybe I was supposed to marry Nick."

"You don't mean that," Joy said painfully. For all her thrilling heart's conclusion, it was Diana's last words that stuck in Joy's head. "You love Kevin and Kevin loves you."

"I feel like I can't breathe," Diana rasped. "Like there's not enough air..."

"I'll open a window." Joy rushed to her feet.

Diana flung herself up. "No... I think I want to go outside."

"I'll go with you," Joy said, her thoughts returning entirely to her sister and the misery she was experiencing.

"Is Kevin still here?" Diana asked woodenly. "I don't want to see Kevin. And I don't want to talk to Mom. I don't want to talk to anyone. I want to be by myself and think."

"I'll go see where Kevin is," Joy said, crossing the room to the door. When she opened it she saw Nick leaning against the hall wall.

"Is Kevin still here?" Joy asked, her eyes stinging the minute she saw him.

"No." Nick shook his head.

Joy swallowed hard. "Diana is coming out of her bedroom. She doesn't want to see anyone. She wants to be alone."

"I'll make myself scarce," Nick said, turning to go into his bedroom. But as soon as Joy went back into Diana's room, Nick changed his mind and went into Joy's.

Joy ran her hand softly down Diana's arm. "Kevin left and Mom is downstairs in the kitchen. Are you sure you don't want me to go outside with you?"

"I'm sure." Diana blew her nose into a fistful of tissues.

Joy walked back out to the hall with Diana. She watched from the top of the stairs as her sister left the house, then Joy went into her own bedroom.

Nick was waiting for Joy just inside the door. He put an arm around her waist, pulling her to him, wanting to comfort her, wanting her to comfort him so he could get through his worry about Kevin.

Joy jerked away from him.

"I need you, Joy," Nick whispered.

"Diana needs you," Joy answered hoarsely, then left him to go back into Diana's bedroom. She'd had intentions of closing the door, but he'd followed right on her heels.

Nick closed the door—with a kick of his foot. "You're going to hear me out, Joy. I've had enough of this," he said loudly.

"You'd better listen to what I have to say first," she replied just as firmly.

They stood angrily facing each other in a clash of wills.

"Listen?" Nick roared, not caring how high she'd raised her obstinate chin. "I'm through listening."

"Well, you're going to want to hear this," Joy stormed. "Diana thinks that maybe she should be marrying you."

"Yeah, well... I don't give a damn what Diana thinks. I'm not in love with Diana. I'm in love with you. And I'm going to marry you... if I have to drag you kicking and screaming down the aisle. In fact, the hell with any aisle. Vegas is faster. And we're going on the first plane I can get us on. Now you can pack a bag or not..."

Nick stopped short then, but only because she hadn't said anything to refute him.

"What if I want a wedding?" Joy asked, winding her arms around his neck. It was exactly the way she'd explained it to Diana. When it was love, you just knew it—with your heart. And when he picked you above anyone else...

It was a second before Nick regained the power of speech. "Baby, if you just said yes to me, you can have anything you want."

Joy put a teasing mouth almost against his. "What took you so long?"

"I was busy running around in circles," Nick countered, then he put that smart, sassy mouth of hers to much better use.

"I love you, Nick," Joy uttered, breaking away from the kiss, basking in the most wonderful moment of her life, her heart all-knowing and settled.

"I love you," Nick murmured, kissing her neck, then gazing playfully into her eyes. "I should be mad at you for putting me through the wringer."

"*Are* you mad?" She was at her impish best while she asked it.

"No, but I am mad about you." Nick grinned. "Are you going to trust everything I say to you from now on?"

"Yes," Joy answered, raining kisses of apology on his chin, on his nose, on his mouth.

"I'll keep proving it to you, anyway," Nick told her. "I'm glad Diana gave me the chance to prove it to you now."

"Oh, God! Diana," Joy moaned.

"Kevin . . ." Nick issued his own troubled sigh. "He's outside walking around."

Joy's fingers dug into Nick's shoulder. "Diana's outside walking around. Do you think they might have run into each other?"

"I think we should go out and see." Nick took Joy's hand.

"How far could they have gone?" Joy asked anxiously, after they'd spent more than a half hour walking all the way to Main Street, looking into a nearby bar, a coffee shop, a luncheonette, then going back to the house.

"I don't think either of them would walk all that far," Nick said, leading her up the driveway.

Joy squeezed Nick's hand. "I'm getting very worried. Should we walk through the woods behind the house?"

"You can stop worrying," Nick said with a chuckle as he glanced inside Kevin's car. Using a hand, Nick turned Joy's head in the direction his eyes had gone.

Joy saw for herself what had brought on Nick's chuckle.

Diana and Kevin were locked in each other's arms as they sat in the back seat, kissing hungrily.

Nick knocked on the window. He had to knock more than once before Diana and Kevin drew apart.

Kevin opened the car door with a grin on his face. "We're okay."

"We're getting married," Diana said, her smile as wide as Kevin's as they both got out of the car.

"I'll put on more hamburgers," Emily Mackey said a while later, as she happily bounced to her feet. "And more potatoes."

"Mom," Diana said with a contented smile, "I couldn't eat another mouthful."

"I'm stuffed." Joy put a hand to her stomach.

"Nothing more for me," Kevin said, one arm around Diana's shoulders, which was the way he'd eaten his meal.

"I couldn't get another thing down," Nick agreed.

Emily sniffled. "My little girl is getting married," she said, as if she was just realizing it.

Nick winked at Joy. Neither had said anything yet about their relationship, leaving the limelight to Diana and Kevin.

"Your other little girl is getting married, too," Nick said casually.

Emily Mackey looked baffled.

"Me, Mom." Joy laughingly pointed to herself. "I'm marrying him." She pointed to Nick.

In a flurry of commotion, everyone spoke at once.

"My baby!" Emily Mackey exclaimed over and over again.

"I had my money on you," Kevin said, slapping Nick's back.

"When?" Diana asked.

"Soon," Joy answered.

"We could get married together," Diana said, bursting with enthusiasm.

"I like that idea," Nick offered.

"Diana, it's *your* wedding," Joy said, shaking her head. "It's *your* special day."

Diana smiled. "You've had as much to do with putting this wedding together as I have. And we'd never forget each other's anniversary. And there's an extra wedding gown upstairs. And we're sisters. And Kevin and Nick are brothers. And the same people that are coming to my wedding would come to yours. Just think how thrilled Uncle Paul will be to walk both his favorite nieces down the aisle."

"The staff from the paper will show up," Nick said, taking up where Diana left off. "I'll make it an order. And we'll call anyone else we want here. I'll want my friend Teddy for my best man. I happen to know he has a tux in his closet. I borrowed it once."

"I wouldn't have to buy a second mother-of-the-bride dress," Emily Mackey added, smiling with tears of happiness in her eyes.

Kevin said, "There's no reason you won't be able to get your blood test quickly. The license won't be a problem, I have connections." He paused a moment. "We might need more food."

"We'll get pizzas if we have to," Nick kidded. "Some with anchovies."

"My two babies..." Emily Mackey blew her nose into a napkin.

"What can I say?" Joy put her hands up in the air.

"It better be yes," Nick said eloquently, his eyes smiling into Joy's eyes.

"Yes," Joy said loudly. "Yes, yes, yes."

"Oh, Diana," Joy breathed. "You've never looked more beautiful."

"Look at you," Diana said admiringly, as the two stood in front of the full-length mirror in Joy's bedroom—both clad in their wedding gowns.

Joy smiled. "I thought I was going to have to put some socks in the top, but Mom took it in."

"And the length is just right," Diana said, laughing. "I wouldn't be surprised now if Nick had designs all along of getting you into this gown. Kevin told me how hard Nick had been working to get you to believe he loved you."

Joy grinned. "I can tell you for sure he has designs about getting me out of this gown."

"I know that I was a naysayer, but I didn't understand what was going on. Why didn't you believe that he loved you?" Diana asked.

Joy sighed wistfully. "I kept comparing myself to you. Diana, you are gorgeous, sophisticated and brilliant."

Her sister looked shocked. "You've got so much more going for you than I have. Do you know how many times I've wanted to clobber you because I've never been able to be as cute as you are?"

"You've wanted to clobber me!" Joy's eyes grew bigger. "I can't tell you how many times I've wanted to clobber you. Do you know how many guys I lost after they took a look at you?"

"What guys?" Diana asked, furrowing her brow. "I never dated any guy you went out with."

"You didn't have to date them. Do you remember Danny Mitchell?" Joy pointed a finger. "The only reason he kept coming around was to stare at you."

Diana's eyebrows came together in a frown. "I don't remember any Danny Mitchell. When was he around?"

"When I was fourteen."

"You had braces on your teeth when you were fourteen."

"Exactly." Joy nodded her head. "Did you ever have to wear braces?" Joy shook her head. "No."

"I wished I had. You had Mom and Dad fussing all over you when you first got them on."

Emily Mackey appeared in the doorway along with Rachel Harmon, who was now Joy's maid of honor, and Tracie Cooper, who was now Diana's maid of honor.

"Are the two of you ready?" the mother of the brides asked, gazing lovingly and teary-eyed at both her daughters. "The limousine is here with your uncle Paul."

"I just have to get my bouquet from my room," Diana answered. "Mom, you look beautiful."

"You do, Mom," Joy echoed emotionally.

"Hurry up," Emily Mackey ordered self-consciously, then led Rachel and Tracie away from the door.

"I'm glad now that I committed to red and white flowers," Diana smiled. "You were right that it should look like Christmas."

Joy hugged Diana.

"Don't let the bedbugs bite," Joy whispered.

"Don't let them bite you, either," Diana whispered back.

Reverend Easton smiled brightly at the two brides. "I've known Diana and Joy since they were born, so it feels quite appropriate that I should be the one conducting this double ceremony today."

Reverend Easton's gaze went to the mother of the brides in the front pew along with the uncle who had given them away and the rest of the immediate family before encompassing the entire assembly. "I welcome you all on behalf of Diana and Kevin and Joy and Nick to witness this day the taking of vows of marriage and family, one woman to one man and one man to one woman in fidelity and love."

Reverend Easton's eyes returned to the nuptial couples. "I ask you now to bow your heads in prayer."

When Joy raised her head she looked into Nick's sparkling blue eyes. He looked back into her glittering gray-green eyes and took her hand.

Joy heard little of Kevin's and Diana's vows, but she was all ears when, in his turn, Nick spoke clearly for all to hear.

"I, Nick, take thee, Joy, for my wife. To love. To honor. To cherish in sickness and in health, forsaking all others until death do us part. I promise you love."

Joy tightly squeezed Nick's hand. "I, Joy, take thee, Nick, for my husband. To love. To honor. To cherish in sickness and in health, forsaking all others until death do us part. I give you my heart.''

"The rings?'' Reverend Easton asked.

Teddy Falco brought forth a gold wedding band as did Kevin's best man.

Nick placed the gold band on Joy's finger. "With this ring, I thee wed.''

Reverend Easton looked first to Diana and Kevin, then to Joy and Nick. "With the power vested in me, I now pronounce you each husband and wife. You may kiss your brides.''

"How much longer do we have to stay?'' Nick whispered in Joy's ear as they danced at the reception. The party was still in full swing, though it was now hours since it had begun.

"Anxious?'' Joy teased.

"Yes, wife. I'm anxious.''

"Good.'' Joy kissed the corner of Nick's mouth. "Me, too.''

"Baby, I'm sorry we can't have a real honeymoon now,'' Nick said. "I'll make it up to you as soon as we can get away.''

Joy smiled. "I have a feeling you're going to make it as much a honeymoon as I can handle.''

"You've got my word on that.'' Nick winked.

Diana and Kevin danced up alongside Joy and Nick.

"I'm going to be changing in a minute,'' Diana said. "We have a plane to catch. Do you want to throw your bouquet with me?''

"Yes, she does,'' Nick answered, while Joy grinned.

"Nick…'' Joy giggled. "You can put me down now. We're over the threshold.'' They were in a hotel room on Shelter Island—a short ferry ride away from Greenport and the newsroom where they were going to have to appear sometime the next day.

He bent his head closer to hers, a suggestive glint in his eyes. "You can ask sweeter than that. Ask me sweet."

Her lips made the request, but Joy didn't use words.

"Anything else?" Nick quipped.

"Nothing comes to mind," Joy answered flippantly.

"Nothing?"

"Do you want me to say I love you?" Joy parried.

"Not if I have to pull it out of you, I don't."

"I love you," Joy whispered. "I love you, I love you, I love you."

"Better." Nick smiled, letting Joy down to her feet.

She unbuttoned her coat with unsteady fingers in anticipation of what lay in store. Her head was already spinning, and the honeymoon hadn't officially started.

Nick took his leather jacket off and flung it on a chair. He put his hand into the pocket of his slacks and came out with a small jeweler's box.

"We didn't have a chance to be engaged, and the jeweler didn't have this ready until yesterday."

In one motion Nick opened the lid. "It's as close as I could come to giving you the moon and the stars." He took her left hand and fitted the ring next to her wedding band. "I remember you once said something about being responsive to the moon, the stars and the sun."

Joy's eyes were blurry as she gazed at a moonstone surrounded by small diamonds, glistening as brightly as any sun.

She wildly kissed the side of his neck and then his mouth while he slipped her coat down her arms. He tossed her coat over his on the chair, then stood back just far enough to see all of her.

She was wearing a crimson red suit without a blouse.

"Red?" Nick grinned, his eyes adoring her.

"Red," Joy answered breathlessly, the color reflected in her cheeks as Nick unbuttoned her jacket, exposing a brand-new red bra.

*   *   *   *   *

AVAILABLE THIS MONTH FROM SILHOUETTE ROMANCE®

#1198 MAD FOR THE DAD
Terry Essig

#1199 HAVING GABRIEL'S BABY
Kristin Morgan

#1200 NEW YEAR'S WIFE
Linda Varner

#1201 FAMILY ADDITION
Rebecca Daniels

#1202 ABOUT THAT KISS
Jayne Addison

#1203 GROOM ON THE LOOSE
Christine Scott

Take 4 bestselling love stories FREE

Plus get a FREE surprise gift!

Bestselling Author

MAGGIE
SHAYNE

Continues the twelve-book series—FORTUNE'S CHILDREN—
in **January 1997** with Book Seven

A HUSBAND IN TIME

Jane Fortune was wary of the stranger with amnesia who
came to her—seemingly out of nowhere. She couldn't deny
the passion between them, but there was something
mysterious—almost dangerous—about this compelling
man…and Jane knew she'd better watch her step….

MEET THE FORTUNES—a family whose legacy is greater than
riches. Because where there's a will…there's a *wedding!*

FC-7

He's able to change a diaper in three seconds flat.
And melt an unsuspecting heart even more quickly.
But changing his mind about marriage might take some doing!
He's more than a man...

He's a FABULOUS FATHER!

***

January:

MAD FOR THE DAD by Terry Essig (#1198)
Daniel Van Scott asked Rachel Gatlin for advice on raising his nephew—
and soon noticed her charms as both a mother...*and* a woman.

February:

DADDY BY DECISION by Lindsay Longford (#1204)
Rancher Jonas Riley proposed marriage to Jessica McDonald! But
would Jonas still want her when he found out a secret about her
little boy?

March:

MYSTERY MAN by Diana Palmer (#1210)
50th Fabulous Father! Tycoon Canton Rourke was a man of mystery,
but could the beautiful Janine Curtis find his answers with a lifetime
of love?

May:

MY BABY, YOUR SON by Anne Peters (#1222)
Beautiful April Bingham was determined to reclaim her long-lost child.
Could she also rekindle the love of the boy's father?

***

Celebrate fatherhood—and love!—every month.
FABULOUS FATHERS...only in ▼ *Silhouette* ROMANCE™

Five irresistible men say "I do" for a lifetime of love
in these lovable novels—our Valentine to you in February!

I'M YOUR GROOM

#1205 *It's Raining Grooms* by Carolyn Zane
After praying every night for a husband, Prudence was suddenly
engaged—to the last man she'd ever expect to marry!

#1206 *To Wed Again?* by DeAnna Talcott
Once Mr. and Mrs., Meredith and Rowe Worth were now adoptive
parents to a little girl. And blessed with a second chance at marriage!

#1207 *An Accidental Marriage* by Judith Janeway
Best man Ryan Holt never wanted to be a groom himself—until a
cover-up left everyone thinking he was married to maid of honor
Kit Kendrick!

#1208 *Husband Next Door* by Anne Ha
When Shelly got engaged to a stable, *boring* fiancé, her neighbor and
very confirmed bachelor Aaron Carpenter suddenly realized *he* was
meant to be her husband!

#1209 *Wedding Rings and Baby Things* by Teresa Southwick
To avoid scandal, very pregnant Kelly Walker needed a husband fast,
not forever. But after becoming Mrs. Mike Cameron, Kelly fell for this
father figure!

Don't miss these five wonderful books,
Available in February 1997,
only from

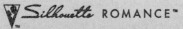

Silhouette ROMANCE™

Look us up on-line at: http://www.romance.net   SR-GROOM

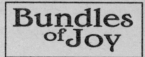

Bundles of Joy

The biggest romantic surprises come in the smallest packages!

January:

HAVING GABRIEL'S BABY by Kristin Morgan (#1199)
After one night of passion Joelle was expecting! The dad-to-be, rancher Gabriel Lafleur, insisted on marriage. But could they find true love as a family?

April:

YOUR BABY OR MINE? by Marie Ferrarella (#1216)
Single daddy Alec Beckett needed help with his infant daughter! When the lovely Marissa Rogers took the job with an infant of her own, Alec realized he wanted this mom-for-hire *permanently*—as part of a real family!

Don't miss these irresistible Bundles of Joy, coming to you in January and April, only from

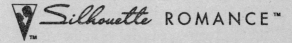

Silhouette ROMANCE™

Look us up on-line at: http://www.romance.net

BOJ-J-A

You're About to Become a

Privileged Woman

Reap the rewards of fabulous free gifts and benefits with proofs-of-purchase from Silhouette and Harlequin books

Pages & Privileges™

It's our way of thanking you for buying our books at your favorite retail stores.

PROOF OF PURCHASE
SR-PP21
Offer expires March 31, 1997

Pages & Privileges ™

Harlequin and Silhouette— the most privileged readers in the world!

For more information about Harlequin and Silhouette's **PAGES & PRIVILEGES** program call the Pages & Privileges Benefits Desk: **1-503-794-2499**

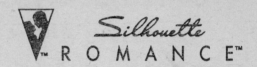

Silhouette
ROMANCE™

COMING NEXT MONTH

#1204 DADDY BY DECISION—Lindsay Longford
Fabulous Fathers
Charming and sexy Jonas Riley had slipped past Jessica McDonald's defenses years ago. Now the rancher was back—and proposing marriage to the single mom. But would Jonas still want Jessica when he found out the secret about her little boy?

#1205 IT'S RAINING GROOMS—Carolyn Zane
I'm Your Groom
Prudence was praying for a husband when rugged Trent Tanner literally fell from above—through her ceiling! Though Trent was no answered prayer, his request that she pose as his fiancée just might be the miracle Prudence was looking for!

#1206 TO WED AGAIN?—DeAnna Talcott
I'm Your Groom
Once Mr. and Mrs., Meredith and Rowe Worth suddenly found themselves adoptive parents to an adorable little girl. Now that they were learning to bandage boo-boos and read bedtime stories, could they also learn to fall in love and wed—again?

#1207 AN ACCIDENTAL MARRIAGE—Judith Janeway
I'm Your Groom
Best man Ryan Holt had never wanted to become a groom himself— until a last-minute cover-up left everyone thinking he was married to maid of honor Kit Kendrick! Now this confirmed bachelor was captivated by lovely Kit and wished their "marriage" was no accident!

#1208 HUSBAND NEXT DOOR—Anne Ha
I'm Your Groom
When Shelly got engaged to a nice, stable, *boring* fiancé, Aaron Carpenter suddenly realized he was in love with his beautiful neighbor, and set out to convince her that he was her perfect husband—next door!

#1209 WEDDING RINGS AND BABY THINGS—Teresa Southwick
I'm Your Groom
To avoid scandal, single mom-to-be Kelly Walker needed a husband fast, not forever. But after becoming Mrs. Mike Cameron, Kelly was soon falling for this handsome father figure, and hoping for a family for always.